★

"IF SANDY IS DEAD, HOW WILL IT MAKE YOU BETTER?"

When a person tells you he plans to kill someone, the options you have for discouraging him are likely to be limited. Especially if you love the person and feel strongly about his grievance, your options are limited. You can assume the casually derisive tone that implies you don't believe him. You can react with the pained horror that shows you very much believe him. You can threaten to alert the police. You can offer to call a therapist. You can invoke a stern morality. You can sympathize with the grievance while condemning the means designed to avenge it.

Actually, when Margaret Berringer's brother David let her in on his plans, she tried all these. A conscientious woman, she stood with one hand on his wheelchair and cried and laughed and argued and implored and preached. She said, David, you're an idiot. She said, Davey, I love you. She said, God knows you're right to be furious. She said, You'd be ruining your own life.

★

"A delicious and tantalizing novel . . . Read it."

—*Best Sellers*

"She develops character as well as suspense without missing a turn of the screw in building tension."

—*Washington Post Book World*

A Forthcoming Worldwide Mystery by
MIRIAM BORGENICHT

BOOKED FOR DEATH

Still Life

MIRIAM BORGENICHT

W🌐RLDWIDE®

TORONTO • NEW YORK • LONDON • PARIS
AMSTERDAM • STOCKHOLM • HAMBURG
ATHENS • MILAN • TOKYO • SYDNEY

STILL LIFE

A Worldwide Mystery/April 1989

First published by St. Martin's Press Incorporated.

ISBN 0-373-26023-7

Printed in U.S.A.

Still Life

ONE

WHEN A PERSON tells you he plans to kill someone, the options you have for discouraging him are likely to be limited. Especially if you love the person and feel strongly about his grievance, your options are limited. You can assume the casually derisive tone that implies you don't believe him. You can react with the pained horror that shows you very much believe him. You can threaten to alert the police. You can offer to call a therapist. You can invoke a stern morality. You can sympathize with the grievance while condemning the means designed to avenge it.

Actually, when Margaret Berringer's brother David let her in on his plans, she tried all these. A conscientious woman, she stood with one hand on his wheelchair and cried and laughed and argued and implored and preached. She said, David, you're an idiot. She said, Davey, I love you. She said, God knows you're right to be furious. She said, You'd be ruining your own life.

"My life is ruined."

"I wish you didn't think that."

"I wish I didn't have to lug around the proof." He gave a brief downward glance; since a year ago last January, he had been paralyzed from the waist down.

"If Sandy is dead, how will it make you better?"

"It won't."

"Well, then . . ."

"I'll stop thinking about ways to hurt him. That'll be better."

"They'll put you in jail."

"A man who can't walk put in jail, that'll be a laugh."

"One of those hospitals, then, that are worse than jail."

"They'll have to catch me first."

"Great. A man in a wheelchair is going to shoot a man on a busy street and they won't be able to catch him."

"Forget that busy street, Maggie. Way I have it set up, no one will know. Except you," he added with a baleful side-long look.

"Hey, David, I'm not the enemy."

"Oh, Maggie, you're a good sister, the best. Don't think I'm not grateful."

"I don't want you grateful, I want you content."

"Would you be content if your life were ruined?" And they were back where they started.

Well, maybe that's what tragedy is all about, she thought: your arguments can never break out of their circular course. Anyhow, it was true of David and her. Whatever the occasion, whether she was on her daily visit to the apartment in the East Eighties that had been done over with scrupulous care for the needs of infirmity, or he was making one of the rare visits to her place, their talk always came around to the fact that a year ago he'd had a good-looking wife and a yacht and a championship rating at his golf club and a partnership in one of Wall Street's more eminent brokerage houses, and now he sat all day in a wheelchair.

Sometimes she thought, What am I doing? Why do I listen so much? Just because I'm two years older and I always adored him—I have my own problems. My own life. I'm not doing him any good, he'd be better off not seeing me so much. But she recognized the self-indulgent nature of this reasoning, and besides, she really was responsible for what had happened. Well, partly responsible. Well, anyhow, involved: she'd recommended the architect whose negligence or maybe you had to say incompetence had caused the accident. "Use Sandy Fleming," she had said when David announced that he and his wife wanted to build a vacation house on Long Island. "What do I know about him? Well, he was wonderful with Erica, you know, he's the one who designed her clinic.'' David had laughed. ''Maggie, sweet, I think it's super that your daughter runs a clinic for rape victims, but what's that got to do with the classy number Patty and I have in mind?'' But he'd looked at work by Sandy and Kenneth Ash, who was his partner, and he must have been impressed because a couple of months and a fair amount of research later he did in fact pick Fleming and Ash. Which led with intractable steps to disaster. Because when some partial framing was up, Sandy and David had driven out to the site at the end of a road that had been picked for its privacy and scenic grandeur, and David had said, ''Okay if I poke around in the cellar?'' and Sandy had said, ''Feel free,'' and David had thereupon picked his way down the temporary steps while Sandy walked out on the planks of what was someday to be a living room but turned out not to be strong enough to support a man. Another inch, as everyone said, and the ensuing crash would have been fatal: this way it was merely tragic.

Well, no matter what anyone thinks, tragedy doesn't breed nobility, it breeds more tragedy. The yacht was refurbished for a new owner, and the golf clubs went to rummage, and the good-looking wife, after months of tearful avowals of love, decided she wasn't cut out for the kind of deprivation this particular injury entailed, and the Wall Street firm painted a new name on its frosted glass door. Which left David with his fury. The only curious thing was that it didn't outwardly show. Faces, she found out, take their time about changing; someone looking at David might still think, what a handsome man, what good strong features and forceful chin and piercing blue eyes, just the way the successful broker in his early forties is supposed to look. But she lived with the truth, which was that rage was steaming inside that prepossessing exterior, riddling him, consuming him. She lived with it because every day he insisted on it, a passionate and unforgiving replay. Any respectable architect would have known the hazard. The beams were not even nailed. He never should have been allowed in that cellar. Sandy was guilty of criminal carelessness. Sandy didn't deserve to live. Over and over in the ferocious voice of a man whose fate defies his powers of accommodation.

Except now, this afternoon, a change. Not just Sandy doesn't deserve to live, Sandy is not going to live, David will kill him.

She looked at him, her personable brother. When they were growing up, in what had been a noncompetitive closeness, they had for a long time been the same size. Twins? people would ask, seeing the two fair-haired children. Cute.

Well, cuteness can go either way—with both of them, it modulated gracefully into attractiveness. David of course emerged as the prototype of the photogenic success story, and after some bumbling years in her late teens she turned out to have the kind of even features and good coloring that are possessed of greater staying powers than some flashier types of beauty.

The closeness held up too, through some strenuous complications in her life and now the crisis in his. Solid affection. But affection doesn't mandate acquiescence. Not when a man loses touch with reality, it doesn't. Not when misfortune is seen as justification for malignity.

"David, honestly, the way you carry on about Sandy. As if he hadn't been hurt himself."

"A broken arm. Big deal."

"I mean, mental suffering," she said, and heard for herself the fatuous note.

"Poor fellow."

"David, I mean it. It . . . well, I happen to know it seared him."

"The hell it did. He's living the same life as before. Buttering up rich clients. Escorting his fat wife to parties. Taking good-looking women to lunch. Good-time Charley."

"Davey, you don't really—"

"And now he's building a house on the same site."

She didn't repress her surprise. "How do you know?"

"I know."

She was silent. From the kitchen, faintly, came the sounds of the man who was preparing his dinner, who would bring it to him, and say, Sure you don't want anything else, Mr. Bynam? and see by his face that attempts at camaraderie were not in order. "David, have you been keeping tabs on Sandy?"

"What else do I have to do?" The sardonic voice he trotted out more and more often these days.

She went over to the window. They'd thought it was so great: modern technology, what couldn't it accomplish? A car designed with exquisite attention to detail and skilled concern for requirements, so one who was without the use of his legs could cross the sidewalk in his motor-impelled wheelchair, and with help from nurse or doorman get suitably seated behind the adjusted steering wheel, and manipulate the adapted accelerator, and then head like anyone else into the sheltering anonymity of city traffic. Freedom for the incapacitated: how they reveled in the idea. Now she realized: license for the infuriated.

"David, a car like that, anyone can recognize it."

"Out there, who'd see it? That glorious site at the end of nowhere, so private, so solitary, nothing but sand dunes all around, don't you remember?"

Well, if someone wants to cultivate bitterness, has made a speciality of refining the nuances of bitterness, no use exhorting him not to be bitter. She came back and sat down and asked whether the old foundation was still standing.

"You mean the house he was doing for us, most goddamn creative design on the Island? The fellow who bought the land from me hired Sandy to build a house for him, that's how much your friend is suffering. He stands on that rock out by the water and broods about it."

She can't let him know how it shocks her. Not the image of Sandy Fleming posed on that rocky ledge but the idea of her own brother practicing the squalid art of concealment so he can be in a position to see that image. "Maybe what Sandy is brooding about is what he did to you."

"Fat chance. He's figuring out another creative design, is what. While I watched he started pacing it out. Twelve steps one way, twenty the other. And you want to know why I didn't kill him that time? Maggie, do you? I didn't have a gun, that's why. Damn fool that I was, I went out there unprepared."

But you have a gun now—what's the use of asking? For someone in his condition, there would be no problem. He could even acquire it legitimately: Yes, that's it, I certainly would be more comfortable at night knowing that if someone broke in . . . a few poignant words, and well-meaning authority would come across with the permit.

She stood looking at him—mouth twisted, hands gripping the wheelchair, useless feet straight on the metal supports. Sometimes friends asked her how she could do it. Honestly, Margaret, a visit every single day, so depressing, purest misery, doesn't it absolutely wear you down?

Well, it wears her down, all right, but not for the reason they think. It wears her down because she is unable to resolve her feelings about him. She listens to the bristling voice and observes the sardonic face and keeps tabs on the meticulous routine needed to keep him alive, and one part of her says he doesn't have to give in to bitterness. Other people overcome handicaps; you read about them all the time. The blind man who graduates from law school. The multiple sclerosis victim who makes it as a doctor. David has brains, God knows, and all the money he needs—he could rise to heroism. Or at least work at keeping his character intact. For his own sake he could. He could put his indubitable talents into creating some kind of career of usefulness. All this vengefulness and self-pity, this obdurate decision to abjure the world, it's himself he's destroying.

But the other part of her looks at him, dressed in the dapper clothes he still goes in for, and thinks, My God. A man of forty-four, never again to make love to a woman. Never stride in his male glory across a room. Never savor the brash athletic triumphs. And not because of some freakily malevolent act of nature, not even the creditable comfort of having performed some act of valor or daring. But to be crippled because some fool architect didn't bother to take the most elementary precautions, well, you can't blame him. Him of all people, what did he ever do to deserve to have life cut off, so now let him get his kicks any way he wants.

Only not when it means murder. "David, it's an insane idea. If you ever did go through with it, you couldn't live with yourself afterwards, you know that. Stop thinking about it, I beg you."

"Mag, don't get all worked up."

"It's you who— Listen. Just because Sandy was alone out there that once... Architects don't drive a hundred miles so they can commune with themselves. They plan to meet contractors, surveyors, clients, I don't know, engineers. I mean, the idea that you can do this, actually track a man down when he's by himself, and maneuver your car so you're in position to shoot him—"

"If I can't, why are you so worried?"

"Besides, you'd never get away with it. Detectives...the police..."

That look of insolent omniscience on his face—maybe in the old days it signaled some emanation of power and insight. I'm in charge. Never mind what the stock market does, the other brokers fear, the press says—leave it all to me. Now what it means is, What do I have to lose, how can things be worse than they are already?

"David, I'm trying to see it your way, really I am. So, okay, the way it looks, you're working on this absolutely misguided premise. You have the idea that killing Sandy would somehow free you, liberate you from your misery. As if, I don't know, an act of that kind of vengeance could negate the fact of impairment. But what you don't realize, if you went through with it, your conscience would drive you mad. Oh, don't make a face—it's true. You wouldn't be liberated, my muddle-headed brother. You'd be suffocated by self-hate. Even assuming you could get away with it. You'd never live down the guilt. It's too out of character. David, believe me, you'd be a wreck, a moral mess, and I just won't let that happen."

It was a longer speech than she'd planned to make, longer than she was in the habit of making, and having worked up momentum, she kept going. "How will I stop it? I'll steal your car, that's what. I'll tell them at the garage never to bring it to you. I'll go there one night and smash it."

"Take it easy, Maggie."

"You think I'm kidding, I can't go in for drastic measures too?"

He reached over to pat her knee. "Hey, Mag, tell me about Erica. What's she up to, that darling girl? How's the clinic? Do they need money?"

She took a breath. See, this proves it, he doesn't mean it. He was just breaking out, a wild aberration, the only kind of project available to give him gratification, which is a fantasy one.

Okay, then, the heartwarming subject of Erica. "Things actually are going all right. The one trustee who was holding out has come around, and the board voted her a new stipend, so it looks as if just about the whole hospital is now behind her. And they took on another staff member. Part-time GYN doctor with psychiatric training, what a windfall, to help with the groups. And with all that she still leads her own life. There's a new man, not serious, but still—"

"How about you, Maggie?"

"Well, of course, I'm for it. The clinic, that is. Even if it still seems to me unreal. Girl of twenty-four, *beautiful* girl of twenty-four, for her to be running the place women turn to at what's absolutely the most desperate moment of their lives, but if that's what she—"

"I mean, what about your prospects? When are you going to get married again?"

The kind of intrusion, nosy but kindly, they have always made into each other's lives. Actually, though he must never suspect this, it was due to him her marriage had broken up. Oh, over the years there had been other problems, of course. When Alex wanted to move to the suburbs and she clung with passionate tenacity to the city. When a couple of years after Erica's birth she decided to quit being a perfect housewife and become a hard-working businesswoman. When Alex slid into the casebook depression of the man hitting forty. And when it came to her that Alex was having an affair with the beautiful woman his factory had hired as their efficiency expert. Each of these had undermined the structure a little. A nip here, a nip there. So maybe it wasn't fair to say David's accident was the cause. Maybe it was the injured feeling she would always sustain after that affair. Maybe it was the grievance stirring meanly in Alex's breast because she had won the city/suburb battle.

But it was David on those last days he talked about. "I feel as bad as you do, Margaret. After all, he was my friend. My friend, if you want to be precise about it, before I became your husband. I loved that guy. Christ, the ski trips, the yachting expeditions. If cutting off my right arm would help. But you don't see me ruining my life for him. Well, sure, I visit him. I'd go more if I thought it would make him happy. But you know what it's like. He asks have I been playing tennis. How was golf last Sunday? He's out to torment himself. Someone scratching the scab. So I pace my visits. Once in a while during the week, sometimes on Sunday. But you, this mindless absorption, so it's the most im-

portant thing in your life. No, Maggie, let me finish. It's like
a religion. Holy observance. Well, suppose you didn't go
one day. Would his housekeeper rear up and leave? Would
that famous urinary tract of his know the difference? Moderation, Maggie, moderation. Maybe he doesn't even want
you to come; that last time we were there when he stormed
at you because the new wheelchair didn't work properly—
maybe it's not even good for him, Maggie, you ever think
of that? But no, every day, every goddamn single day. And
he doesn't appreciate it, you told me yourself. No such thing
as trying to make it easy for you, just the opposite. Five-
thirty, his sister shows up, that's the signal to let loose all the
gripes. So when you come home, how do you think it is for
me? This zombie walking in. Seven days a week I sit down
to dinner with it. David and the new braces. David and the
changed diet. David and his bowels. I'm married to a com-
bination trained nurse and social worker."

Well, a couple of months later, they were not married.

Now she said to David there was no man on the horizon.

"There was six months ago. That snappy fellow, adver-
tising, wasn't he, his heart on his sleeve. And the month
before that, the hotshot lawyer..."

"Oh, well."

"Hell, Maggie. Good-looking woman like you, a year
since you've been alone, you weren't cut out to be a nun."

She stood up and said she didn't exactly lead a nunlike
existence, she had to run now but one of these days she
would give him particulars, and meanwhile she'd be at a
bookstore tomorrow, she'd hunt up those books he wanted
and bring them. Lightly, lightly, the only way it's possible
to speak when his eagle eyes are watching because he knows
as well as you do that into a loving and protective and
tremulous relationship a whole new reason for ambivalence
has been interjected.

Murder: he doesn't mean it. He's spouting the kind of
daydream immobility will invariably foster. But he would

never translate it into action, never. After all, her own brother, someone with his fundamental goodness and magnanimity, for him actually to load a gun, and track down another man's movements, and keep a stealthy distance behind that man's car on the drive out, and wait with nervy patience for the moment when the putative victim is exposed, for him to gear himself to a project so ugly and brutal and out of character... impossible.

He does mean it. The iron core of purposefulness is there. A fundamentally good man, yes, but interminable brooding can change someone, it's folly to pretend otherwise. For a year he has concentrated on a ruinous accident while seeing its agent walk around unscathed and presumably untroubled...the resulting fury has tipped him over. Oh, the lovable David may still be there, sweetly bemused about a niece, honestly concerned about a sister, but underneath the idea of inequity grinds away, deluding him that comfort is to be obtained in the fact of someone else's disaster. Even when he calls her nunlike it's himself he's thinking of, that wondrous apparatus put permanently out of commission, well, of course he's ready to strike back in the only way open to him.

Which is it? Does he mean it or is he just talking? She can't ask him, can't risk augmenting the danger by seeming to take seriously the threat. And besides, she thought as she bent to kiss him good-bye, there is just a chance he doesn't know the answer himself.

TWO

SANDY AND MYRA Fleming lived in a four-story Federal-type house on a pleasant street in Greenwich Village, the kind of place that tells you as soon as you walk in that an architect's sensibility has been at work. You know someone has worked at arriving at that particular color of gray-green for the walls, and said, No, another inch, when workmen were cutting out the arch, and discarded twelve samples of olive wood before finding the one for the bookshelf, and as an afterthought, as the photographer was ready to snap the picture, tossed the orange pillow to soften the austere line of the couch.

Myra Fleming was on the couch when Margaret walked in, but she wasn't erect on it, she sat in the kind of graceless slump that the exacting sensibility could not have had in mind. Her looks weren't exactly what it would have ordered either. She was a little too soft. Fat, David had said, but flabby was more like it. Pretty features, but they didn't have the crispness to go with well-ordered lines and subtle colors.

Or maybe, Margaret thought, it's her expression, that enervated look that pulls at her nice brown eyes and makes her shoulders droop and her mouth sag as she talks. "I was so pleased when you called. If you knew the number of times this spring I've thought about calling you. So does it mean your brother isn't angry at Sandy anymore?"

Margaret gave a tight smile and said her visit didn't mean exactly that.

"Anyhow, you and I can, I hope, be friends. Because a tragedy like that, we're in it together, aren't we? What I mean is, we all feel terrible about it. Sandy, of course, but me too. I never stop thinking about your brother. Sometimes when we pass someone on the street, someone who's you know crippled, my heart absolutely stops. For Sandy the pinch comes from the opposite. It's when he seen someone like your brother used to be, one of those strapping men swinging a golf club or climbing with one easy motion out of a pool, that's when it gets to him. He breaks down and cries like a baby. You may not believe it, but he does."

"David doesn't want people crying about him." She said it the more firmly in that, like every other aspect of his infirmity, there was ambivalence here as well. Sometimes he said, Why shouldn't everyone else suffer too, let them feel guilty, the bastards, serve them right. Sometimes, on the other hand, a natural sweetness asserted itself and he exuded a sincere goodwill. Were his guests enjoying themselves? Any special little thing he could order for them? Food holding up okay?

"Would you like a drink? Coffee, then? Tea? You're sure? Well, how is he, your brother?" Myra asked. "Oh, I don't mean physically, Lord knows I realize. I mean, his mental state. For instance, is he involved in any, um, activity? They do say if people like that keep themselves occupied."

He's not people like that. He's David. Unique. She felt herself bridling inside. For this second, sitting here next to the wife of the man who injured him, she herself is David, she has appropriated his resentments, his self-destructive anger, his irrational pride.

"He's not working, if that's what you mean. He had one of those powerhouse jobs before the accident. Partner in I guess one of the biggest brokerage houses. Oh, I know, I know, they could arrange transportation, fix up his office, special equipment, all that. But not for him. It's not the kind of job, he says, where a man who's paralyzed could function."

Myra Fleming sat with chin sunk on chest. "Maybe some lesser job."

"He wouldn't take a lesser job, why should he, that's not what he's cut out for." Still bridling, offering to this woman all the arguments David with his pained scorn has showered on her.

The soft chin tilted briefly up. If business wasn't the answer, maybe some other kind of interesting work. People with similar problems getting together. "They say it really is helpful in situations like that. People talking to others in the same boat. Like mothers with retarded children. Or, you know, people who've been exposed to one of those horrid chemicals. The group has meetings and votes for officers and runs benefits, things like that, so if your brother—No? He wouldn't consider it? Now you're offended, aren't you?

Yes, actually, she is.

"Don't be," Myra said. "I didn't mean anything wrong."

True enough. She would never mean anything wrong. She would just sit there with her plaintive expression, her graceless pose, her soft air of inertia, and something of impalpable wrongness would issue from her well-intentioned mouth.

Then rueful, awkward, she would try to make amends. "Maybe that kind of thing isn't for everyone. I suppose there are experts who know about that, aren't there?"

Yes, indeed.

"People who understand the needs of different kinds of patients. Must be interesting," she said absently. "To be able to give that kind of advice. Sometimes I think if I'd gone in for something like that instead of what I did do..."

She paused, waiting for the obligatory question, and after a second, Margaret obliged.

"Oh, I'm a painter. Sandy never mentioned it? I have been for years. All my life, just about. No, that's not my picture." She spoke with vague regret, twisting her hand around the orange pillow. "Not that one either. Mine are all in my studio. It's upstairs, a sensational room with this great window—want to see it? Don't say yes if you don't mean it. But some other time, maybe?''

Surely some other time, Margaret said, because what she has to say can get no help from the setting of Myra's sensational studio.

"Why wouldn't it be a great room, Sandy's design, after all. Well, you know all about that, look at the job he did on your daughter's clinic."

Margaret sat straight. She has to offer some congratulatory comment. After all her ungracious demurrers, time for her to give an inch. No, David, I am not being traitorous. This is basic courtesy. "It was wonderful of Sandy to do that for Erica," she said.

"Well, that clinic, such a worthwhile project." Myra slumped lower on the unyielding couch. "You must be very proud of your daughter."

Yes, she certainly is.

"She must be very competent, running a place like that. After all, when you think of the problems."

Yes, lots of problems.

"Only thing, for someone so young, just twenty years old, to be handling that kind of subject matter."

Oh, Myra. Saying the wrong thing, as usual. Margaret said Erica was twenty-four.

"Even so. A girl that age to be hearing details like that. The women must be full of it, how they fought back and what the man threatened and their exact feelings while it was going on and the suffering afterwards. I mean, for her to sit there and take it all in."

Now she knows. It's not that Myra says the wrong thing. She says what others think and have the sense to keep to themselves. "Someone has to sit there."

"Oh, definitely. But your own daughter. And you don't object? You don't sometimes wish she were doing something else, some other kind of job? You must be a very strong woman.''

I'm a weak woman. I can't bring myself to say what I've come for. I acquiesce while she goes on and on, dogma from that omniscient They about the way David should lead his life and misguided talk about Erica and clumsy passes at friendship, and I can't get to it. Maybe I should have said yes to a drink; you need to be a little tipsy to handle a subject like the one I'm burdened with.

If only it were possible to come out with the truth. My brother wants to kill your husband. Sandy is in danger. Myra, you're in big trouble... With no evasions or obfuscations, the distasteful fact laid out in this room where every object has been chosen for what it can contribute to the tasteful and well-ordered and interesting look.

But she can't do that to David. For an idea carved out of desperation, a daydream, a fantasy, she can't brand him a murderer. Or at least not to anyone except the putative victim. But neither can she take chances. A word to Sandy, then: all that is needed. Don't go out there alone. The simplest of precautions, to deter the most unlikely of threats.

All right, then, get it under way. She put down her cup and said she wanted to talk to Sandy, who she understood was in Chicago—anyhow, that's what his office had said— so if Myra would tell her how to get in touch with him.

The brown eyes widened. ''That's why you came? To track down Sandy?''

''Myra, there's something important I want to ask him. A favor for me.'' The phrase heartened her, and she repeated it. For me: how literally true. Not primarily to save this woman's husband from injury, but to save my own brother from destroying himself.

Myra looked at her sharply. This something to ask Sandy—was it to do with David?

''Well, yes. I suppose—yes, it surely is.'' Oh, Lord, why can't she get on with it. ''Thing is, I need Sandy's help.''

Help: the impasse-breaking word. Myra waved a vague hand. "He'll be back Saturday. I'll have him call you right away."

She coughed: not fair that it should be so hard. "You don't understand. I have to talk to him before he comes back." Before he takes it into his head to go from the airport directly to that site on Long Island where there is just a chance David will be waiting with his newly purchased gun. "Myra, listen. There's this company right outside Chicago, well, two men, really, they're working on the kind of therapeutic swimming pool you could put right into an apartment. Oh, not a real swimming pool, don't get me wrong, more like a grandiose tank. For someone like David, patients, you know, with spinal cord injuries, part of the basic treatment is that they get upright every day. To help the circulation. 'Ensure the normal gravitational stimuli,' in that awful technical language. And you can do it by getting into braces, but they're horrendous affairs, David hates them, that half hour he spends standing in them is a punishment. So if he could keep himself vertical simply by getting into water..."

Sounded a great idea, Myra said.

"Well, it's just at the beginning stages, something that would fit into a room and get by all the apartment house regulations and building codes and so on—even the journals that usually look into this stuff haven't written it up. So what I want Sandy to do—"

"He always says if he could help he'd feel better."

"So if he could appraise this outfit, see if they're reliable, what kind of setup and financing...questions like that. They need money to go further, is what I heard, but I don't want to mention it to David, get him interested until—"

"You could trust Sandy to get you the lowdown."

"Anyhow, you can see I need to talk to him," Margaret said. "So if you'd tell him—when will you speak to him?"

"Tonight," Myra said. "He usually calls between six and seven so if I go out—not that I do go out very much—that way we won't miss each other."

Margaret nodded and reached for her purse. She was really grateful. Such a big help. Tell Sandy she'll be waiting to hear.

"Suppose he doesn't call?"

"What?"

"I mean"—Myra raised the flabby cheeks—"he just might not. He might be busy. Or have an appointment. He's at this conference. Housing for the Homeless, architects from all over the country. But he might also be seeing this client, well, not really a client yet. Someone who's thinking about moving his business to New York. Sandy took out a couple of sketches in case the man decides to use Fleming and Ash for the job. So if he wants to see Sandy at just six o'clock . . ."

"Okay, then, I'll call him. Simple. Just tell me which hotel." Margaret stood up. But though she waited, the conspicuously departing guest, Myra remained in her torpid pose.

"I know which hotel he had reservations at, naturally I do. But he's funny about hotels. A perfectionist. I remember once we had to leave some really nice place, just check out at seven at night and find something else because the color of the walls didn't go with the rug, it bothered him. Oh, it's fine that he has such high standards, it's what makes him a terrific architect, but then when you don't know which hotel."

All right, it's not so simple. "You mean, he might have moved?"

Myra pushed back her hair. That was exactly what she meant. "But then again, he might not. He's, well, unpredictable. You can't be sure. If I could get a list of all the hotels in Chicago and try them one by one."

All these obstacles—for a second she was tempted to drop it. After all, so slight a danger: that a man coming home from a business trip would decide to go directly to a construction site fifty miles distant, and that he would get there at just the moment when another man was waiting.

That conference, she said. Couldn't he be paged there?

"But suppose he doesn't go. He knows lots of people in Chicago. Suppose he spends all his time talking to them. Oh, no one realizes what a hard profession it is, how people take advantage. We're thinking of turning this old building into a nursery school, they say, what do you think? And the architect says, well, you could extend this space in back and take down that wall and cut an atrium here to bring light into this lower floor—ideas like that. And the client, the prospective client, he says, very interesting, and half the time he takes the ideas and goes to another architect. Or once he has the ideas, he figures he doesn't need an architect at all, he can work it out himself with a builder. And meanwhile all that waste of time, talking and drawing up sketches..."

Myra kneaded the orange pillow. "It's not like lawyers. Sandy doesn't complain, but lawyers have it easy, he says so himself. Like his brother Simon—imagine if someone would say to Simon, if we retain you for this case, tell us what kind of brief you'll be writing." The mournful brown eyes looked up. Margaret knew Simon, didn't she?

"I know Sandy has got him to take pro bono cases for the clinic. Erica couldn't be more grateful."

"Yes. A stupendous man. Very successful. That's lawyers for you, the money rolls in, Sandy says."

She's babbling. Something has set her off. Margaret put down her purse and sat again.

"Being a painter, that's not such a pushover either. I'm not a bad painter, really I'm not. But you know how many not-bad painters there are right here in New York? How many new ones come out of the art schools every year? All

of them with the right courses and the best teachers and that
year in Paris behind them? Ah, well, someday maybe I'll
click. Sandy says I should keep at it. He says I definitely
have something. Especially the landscapes I'm doing now.
The floral studies last year were good, but these are better,
more my thing; he says I definitely shouldn't quit.''

Myra put the pillow back on the couch. ''Life's a mess,
isn't it,'' she said. ''Here I am, all those paintings piled up
in my studio, and Sandy out there someplace where we can't
find him. Such a shame that you had to come here all for
nothing.''

This time Margaret kept standing. ''But it's not for
nothing. Now I know about his program, I'll try his office.
Kenneth Ash, isn't that his partner? Surely he'll have a line
on where Sandy is staying.''

Myra nodded. Ken Ash. Yes. If Margaret really wants to
enlist Sandy for that little project, Ken is the best bet. Does
Margaret know the address? Wait, she'll write it down.

Back to the languid tone and indolent pose again. But the
brown eyes looked anxious and her hand shook as she
wrote, as if in some part of her mind there existed the conviction that Margaret's mission didn't involve any little
project, that it concerned, as the books say, life and death.

THREE

SHE PRESENTED TO KENNETH ASH the same explanation about a therapeutic swimming pool. Something to abet David's circulation without the cruel treatment of his having to stand in the hated braces.

And Ken Ash was even more positive about Sandy's possible contribution. He'd been working in their office, which was on the ground floor of an apartment building on Riverside Drive, but he put down his pencil and said the business of appraising a business venture was right up Sandy's alley. "Close to what he does for us when he works up an estimate. Always a tricky proposition. Come in too low and you lose your shirt. Too high and the competition has you."

He had a long, narrow thoughtful face which turned its frowning gaze briefly on his drawing and then back to her again. Sandy's role he could see, he said. But also he felt sure Sandy would recognize some problems.

"Problems?"

"With a swimming pool in an apartment? Okay, a grandiose tank. Whatever you call it, all that added weight. You'd have to find some way to engage it with the building framework."

"Engage it?" How long is she going to sit here repeating his words?

"You'd have to run beams from one column to another to pick up the vertical load. That's okay if two columns happen to run through your brother's apartment. If only one does, he might have to buy the apartment next door.

Either that or persuade a neighbor to have his life be disturbed for a period of strenuous construction.''

"I see." Why a swimming pool! Why didn't she invent something else!

"Also, of course, space in the apartment below would be needed."

"Well . . ."

"You'd also have to think about the potential disaster of all that water spilling—you'd probably need a second tank inside the first. Sandy would agree with me there, I'm sure."

She sat back. She felt dizzy, disoriented. Like telling someone your dream and hearing it criticized on grounds of faulty logic: But that's impossible, a trunk couldn't suddenly turn into a bird . . . Here he is, this thoughtful man, applying honest-to-goodness structural laws to her fictional construct.

Then another cautionary statement. Such an ambitious project, how would her brother feel about it?

She spoke firmly. In a case like his, all you could do was try everything.

"Still. Something that would be so disruptive. From what I've heard about your brother—well, he's very bitter, isn't he?"

Oh, Lord. Not just an architectural critique of the non-existent project, but a psychological appraisal of the difficult patient. It'll be Myra all over again: the fatuous suggestions about how David should lead his life, the patronizing views on character, the fluent expressions of sympathy.

She heard her icy tone. "He's not just bitter, he's furious. Full of anger."

"I really don't—"

"His life is empty and he's keeping it like that. Empty, empty. He doesn't want them to make some busywork job at his old office because they're sorry for him, and he won't have friends in his apartment every Tuesday so they can pretend to be interested in a course in Restoration Drama, and he doesn't want to be president of Paraplegics for Peace. You look upset. You think he doesn't sound as if he's trying to accommodate. Okay, he's not trying to accommodate.''

''Mrs. Berringer—''

''He's not a nice man these days, that's perfectly true. He's mean-spirited and cranky and boring and vindictive. He's tormented by the idea of unfairness. He thinks everyone should suffer as much as he does; he wants to be around to see the suffering.''

''Mrs. Berringer, look here—''

''He used to be the most concerned of men. If you had a problem, you didn't have to mention it, like a shot he would sense it. He didn't just sense it, he was ready to sit down and listen. What am I saying! He didn't just listen, he'd do something about it. And I don't mean just giving money. He was in there, David himself, pitching for you. Only now...''

''*Listen*. I broke both my legs once. A bad skiing accident when I was nineteen. I wanted to kill the fellow who bumped into me. I knew it was my fault as much as his, but I still wanted to kill him. I had to be in traction for six months, and after that casts up to my hips for another six. When you're nineteen, that's a lifetime. Everything was over for me, I knew it. There was no use going on. I hated everyone, hated myself most of all. So of course your brother... from where he's sitting, life really is over.''

She took a breath. ''I'm sorry. I didn't mean to sound off. It's just, I don't know, thinking about it so interminably.''

He straightened the transparent paper over the drawing. Then he said he understood, only natural.

''It gets to me sometimes.''

''How can it not? Especially being here, in Sandy's office. Look, the moment Sandy calls, I'll tell him to call you.''

All right, finished. An easier mission, after all, than with Myra. This man doesn't have obscure anxieties of his own to get in the way. He did, though, frown briefly and ask why she hadn't gone to Myra. Sandy's wife, after all. Wouldn't she be the obvious source if someone wanted to get in touch with Sandy?

"I did go. I just came from there. She sounded . . ." Margaret paused. How convey that mixture of listless confusion and agitated concern? Besides, Sandy's partner, he surely knows Myra better than she does; sitting here in the checked shirt and gray slacks that are the architect's working costume, he can probably envision the response. "She sounded mixed up. She said Sandy would definitely call but maybe he wouldn't. She knew which hotel he was staying at but then again she didn't know. He'd be at some conference but he might not be there."

When Kenneth Ash frowned, his eyebrows moved together. "Guess this whole thing about your brother has her upset too," he said finally. "God knows, Sandy still can't talk about it without going into a tailspin."

"Fat lot of good that does David." Oh, this is crazy. Taking out her turmoil on this perfectly unoffending man. She sat back and in tacit apology said one reason for her uptight feelings was that she felt herself to be partly responsible.

His hands were folded on his tilted desk. Responsible for what happened? How did she figure that?

"Well, David wouldn't have come to your office if Sandy hadn't done that design for my daughter's clinic. And Sandy wouldn't have done the design if—Do you really want to hear this?"

Yes. He wanted to hear.

"What happened was I met Sandy and Myra one night at a dinner party. I was talking about my daughter, who was trying to get a clinic for rape victims started in one of the city hospitals. Well, rape. You don't mean to hold an entire table spellbound, but no matter how you downplay it the word has a certain mesmerizing quality, and Sandy at the other end of the table must have been listening because after dinner he came up and said if Erica was having trouble he'd like to help—anyhow, that started it.''

She paused; her mind's eye gave her Sandy, his voice eager, his gaze brimming with solicitude and affability both. He was a short man with a round pleasant face, a friendly manner, and a knack of investing whatever he was talking about with zest. Though he wasn't the kind to sound off on memorable subjects, she'd noticed at dinner that whenever he spoke, heads turned, eyes shone, faces nodded with bemused agreement. A charmer. And after dinner, there he was charming her. "Sounds like quite a girl, that daughter of yours," he said. "So if there's anything a run-of-the-mill architect can do."

Well, he wasn't run-of-the-mill, and he found a way to help. What had been a sprawling open space used first as a day-care center for the children of hospital employees and then as a storage depot for hospital files was transformed, with the artful use of partitions and interesting colors and inner stairs, into a dozen attractive offices. Now Margaret looked around. "I suppose you know the nifty design Sandy did for the clinic."

A companionable smile. Yes. Kenneth Ash did know that nifty design.

"Did gratis. You must know that too. Does he do that often, contribute his work without pay?"

"Not on your life. There must have been something about you. Or your daughter. Or, as you say, her project. Architects can't afford to work for nothing. You see our setup. Sandy, me, Joe in there who does drafting, another assistant but she's out now—what I'm saying, Fleming and Ash does all right, probably better than most, but unless you're absolutely at the top, it's not a profession in which you make a mint.''

She stood up. Four small offices, divided by six-foot-high partitions, and all equipped with the same tilted tables, steel cabinets, swivel chairs, gooseneck lamps, drawings. She studied the drawings tacked to Ken's walls and then pointed at random. "A staircase? Looks wonderful. Sort of floating."

"Those steps you think are floating are made with sheets of steel an eighth of an inch thick—these suspension rods and steel stringers hold them up. You didn't notice them? That's sort of the idea, that you shouldn't notice. A staircase that's solidly supported and looks suspended, what we were after."

She followed him along the wall. What about this?

"Oh, that. We entered a competition. College halls, gym, student center—that was our entry. Very classy, don't you think? Just right for small Midwest college with a faintly Gothic theme. P.S. We didn't win.

"We did win this next one, though. A police station. Our idea—you can see—was to evoke authority and also brighten up the neighborhood. Those blue metal panels— they're supposed to remind you of the shiny blue police car. And the triangular plaza—to draw you in, make you feel comfortable. Anyhow, as I say, we did get that one but then they decided they didn't have money enough to go ahead. Luck of the game."

She had the sense of someone talking more than he usually did. She had let loose about David, and now here he was, this unaccustomed burst of information and wry admission. She pointed to another wall: keep it coming.

"This one? No, it's not cells in a jail, just the honeycomb grid to lower a ceiling in an office corridor. But this next is kind of interesting. Critical care unit for a hospital. See, here's the nurses' station, that's the nucleus. The idea is for the nurses to have an unobstructed view—all these diagonals—into every room. We didn't win that one either, but one of the trustees who was outvoted liked our plan so much he hired us to do his vacation home. Over there, house by a lake, those three drawings. Win some, lose some.''

Margaret nodded. In essence, it was what Myra had said: the futile tries, the lost time, the unmerited rejections—occupational hazard. But Ken made it sound intriguing, even gallant: you gambled, you laid your talent on the line, win or lose you had in some indefinable way advanced yourself. When his voice wound down, he busied himself adjusting the glass tacks in another drawing. Then he turned. ''Look here. I don't make much of lunch, just a bite at a place over on Broadway, is there by any chance somewhere you don't have to get in a hurry?''

Well, lunch in a small noisy restaurant for two people who have just met—what wonders can be accomplished beside the mere partaking of food and drink. You sit opposite each other in a corner where the waitress takes her time coming over, and the people at the table on one side are talking too loud about their mortgage, and those at the table on the other side are too incensed at each other to talk at all, and the atmosphere of intense preoccupation is contagious, so what started as an interview slides into something approaching an intimacy. You, him. You don't even have to go through the ritual of Please-call-me, etc., etc.—sometime after the first cocktail it appears you have automatically shifted from Mrs. Berringer to Margaret, while he in the easiest way turns out to be Ken.

Information traded first. She told him where she worked—firm that did marketing research where her specialty was newspapers—and he went on about his current project, which was two floors for a foundation that wanted to attract the money without seeming to be too blatantly in it. And by the time the first course was over, she found herself doing what she rarely did, what she had told herself over and over was impolitic or in bad taste or self-indulgent or even a kind of betrayal to do, which was to talk about David.

"Well, yes, I do go to see him every day. But don't sit there looking at me as if I'm the sweet perfect sister. Sometimes going up in the elevator I feel an absolute spasm of despair, I think I can't make myself open that door, I can't face those reproachful deadened eyes. So why do I go through with it? Because I'd feel even more uncomfortable, all hateful and encumbered with remorse, if I didn't go."

"Awful for you," he said.

"No. It's awful for him." Oh, Lord, there she goes again, that gratuitous snapping. But he nods, he doesn't take offense, he finishes his soup and tells her to go on.

"Listen. I'll tell you just one detail that makes life unbearable. Help. Getting the right people to take care of him. Oh, they're all decent people, I'm sure, but no one's set up to do an impossible job, which is what someone in his condition basically requires." She put down her fork. "No. Requires is wrong. The truth is, someone in his condition doesn't need, might even be better off, without a full-time attendant. But he doesn't want to be independent. You might say he doesn't want to be better off. What he wants is to be what he once was. Failing that, he wants the perks conferred by illness, starting with someone to take care of him every minute. Over one six-month period last year, we had eight changes of staff. They fought with each other, they fought with David and me, one of them stole David's silver loving cups that he'd won at his golf club, one of them really didn't like incapacitated people, one liked them too much, in a way that was even worse, pathologic, really, what a mess till we could boot that one out. What it comes down to, I guess, we need someone who's willing to make another man's infirmity the main interest in life. But someone who's willing to make another man's infirmity the main interest in life isn't the kind of person you particularly want to talk to, much less spend a day with. If you don't want that salad, I'll eat it."

"Feel free."

"I didn't mean to talk so much."

"If it makes you feel better, why shouldn't you?"

She must be feeling better. She polished off the pasta and the two salads and a roll and butter and said, Sure, why not, when he asked about dessert. And she finds she wants to keep talking.

"And if he makes it hard for people to take care of him, it's even worse for those who just want to help him. After the first terrible months in a hospital, he went to a rehabilitation institute. A wonderful place, really. So one thing they institute is activities. For people like him who can use their arms, they try games. Volleyball. Archery. Even basketball in wheelchairs. Oh, I know, it sounds grotesque, but it gives lots of them satisfaction. Only not my brother."

"He didn't want to be part of the group. Another victim of paralysis."

"You're so right. I remember his exact words. 'Maggie, when I want to enter Olympics for the Disabled, I'll let you know.' And it's no better now. Old friends, good friends, they're up against the same frost. And they don't give up, they try everything. Like what? Oh, like I said, can they all get together for a course in his apartment? They'll tackle it all. Archaeology. I don't know. Modern poetry. Expressionist painting. Anything so it's assured that on one night a week he'll be surrounded by concerned faces and lively talk. Or maybe will he teach the course, economics, how to win in the stock market? Or if they fix up their summer house, a complete rehaul, hospital bed, private bathroom, the works, will he come out and visit them? He rebuffs everything. He says he won't be condescended to. Well, they're not condescending, they're trying—"

"To be helpful. I'm sure. But from what I gather, your brother was always the one in command. The number one man. For someone like that, all that attentive helpfulness must sound damn close to condescension."

She nodded. He understands. Has that prickly character figured out.

"Should I tell you the truth? Even that whole bit about his standing up, being vertical—well, it's not strictly essential. Oh, it's good for his cardiovascular system, of course, but that's not what really gets him. What it is, he's deluding himself, thinking if he keeps his muscles in shape he'll be a candidate for something called computerized electrical stimulation, which by emplanting electrodes in the skin will enable people like him to walk. But computerized electrical stimulation, if it turns out to work at all, won't do so for maybe another thirty years, so who's kidding who."

He waited while the people with the mortgage problem made a noisy exit, and then said he'd given some thought to the problem. His wife, his ex-wife, that is, was a no-nonsense psychiatrist with an eclectic practice. Drug addicts. Kleptomaniacs. Victims of incest. Perpetrators of incest...you name it, Alice took them on. But she turned out to be booked up when it came to paraplegics. Too fraught with frustration, she said. Always that moment when it hit the patient that despite all the matters on which he'd been able to come to terms, therapy was still not going to restore his severed spinal cord, put him back in control of his life, so why did he have to go through this three afternoons a week?

Ken leaned across the table. "How about your brother? He ever go in for therapy?"

"He tried about a year ago. To do me a favor, he consented to try. But he knew in advance it wouldn't help so it didn't."

A silence, while the people on the other side made ostentatious passes at what appeared to be a reconciliation. Then Ken said he felt a very real involvement. Sandy's partner, after all. He'd had a hand in designing that unfortunate house, well, he wished there were some way he could get in the act.

She started. Seduced by the easy conviviality, she'd almost forgotten what had brought her here. "Biggest thing you can do is make sure I get in touch with Sandy."

"You really care a lot about this, don't you?"

She really did.

"You don't know anyone else who could look over that swimming pool setup?"

"Not anyone who's on the spot and is up to handling the job."

He pushed his cup and saucer away. Then he said she might think of going to Sandy's brother Simon.

"I don't get it."

"Just to be on the safe side." And when she kept looking puzzled—"Sandy will call the office, of course he will. Routine. But suppose he doesn't. He doesn't call and I can't get him at the places where I know he's working. He's unpredictable. Always had this streak of unpredictability. Maybe it's to do with the artistic temperament. Anyhow, for something that, as you say, means a lot, we don't want to leave any loopholes, do we?"

Unpredictable. The same word Myra had used. Same word, same recantation of previously affirmed positions. Also, same descent into elusive vagueness. She sipped her coffee, making it last, grateful for the cup to conceal her mouth, while his voice went on. Sandy's only brother. Always a close relationship. Even closer now that Simon was up for nomination by his party for congressman. No, not here in the city, the district in Westchester where he lived. She didn't know? Hadn't heard? Chance of his life, what he'd always wanted, had set his heart on.

"He and Sandy talk about it all the time. And I know for a fact there's an errand on Simon's behalf connected with this Chicago trip. Something about getting the promise of money for the campaign from an old family friend. Now I think of it, I heard Sandy promise to call him. 'Sure thing, Simon, as soon as I talk to them, I'll get back to you.'"

"Them. If you know the name you can call him there."

He didn't know the name. Sorry.

She began speaking very fast; she could hear her voice, high pitched, urgent, above the clatter from dishes, chairs, other voices. Why couldn't he leave a message at the conference? Home for Homeless—was that what Myra had said? Surely someone could page him.

His voice, on the other hand, had sunk to a low rumble. He planned to do that, of course. But Sandy was—

"Uh huh. Unpredictable."

"For all I know," Ken said, "he might not even go to the conference. We have a fair number of contacts in Chicago. Good prospects. People who might be considering Fleming and Ash for their next civic center or factory or apartment renovation—Oh, Myra told you, did she? Or, who can say, he might move on to another city." He started on his cake, but without attention, as if his eyes weren't meant to see what his hand was doing. In the same absent tone, he said if this was too hard for her, he'd talk to Simon himself, but all things considered, something that involved her own brother, it was probably best coming from her.

"It's okay. I'll ask him."

"You do know Simon, don't you?"

"Not really. But I know he's tops as a lawyer, and he's been helping Erica. Helping the clinic, that is. Sandy got him into it—yes, didn't you know? From time to time this past year, he's tried cases for them. Tried them gratis, that is. God knows the clinic could never afford the kind of fee a lawyer like him normally charges." She paused; she had once let slip to David the fact of the work that Simon contributed, and David was incensed. For Erica to have anything to do with a member of that family! Even sit in civil parlance with him! David was wrong, of course—Erica, after all, was accepting a favor, not granting a pardon—but in a funny way maybe he also was right. For Sandy's victim to take umbrage because his niece is benefiting from the magnanimity of Sandy's brother—it was a question with the kind of subtle overtones she wouldn't mind discussing with Sandy's partner. But the time for that kind of discussion was past; up ahead—face it!—was another errand. When she stood, she said she saw his point; she'd explain to her office that she wouldn't after all be in at two, and she'd go to see Simon. Meanwhile, she enjoyed the lunch.

Well, that was true. As lunches went, this one rated high: good company, easy talk, food more palatable than she'd been led to expect. But the fact remained that for all the thoughtful interest and superior understanding of her lunch companion, he did the same thing Myra did, which was to pass the buck.

FOUR

SEE SIMON IMMEDIATELY, she had said, but it's never that simple. The telephone operator at his office said Mr. Fleming wasn't in, and it took the intercession of two similar clipped voices, each more insistent on weighing credentials and justifying refusals than the other, before she found out that Mr. Fleming was in court, trying a case on behalf of the Rape Intervention Center.

She opened the door of the phone booth. Damn. She's all for his doing this, thinks it's splendid, public-spirited, generous, decent, but not today, when she would like him to be accessible in some midtown office where you are ushered in courteously, cosseted tactfully, induced with the most practiced affirmations of helpfulness to talk. All right, then, another call.

"Erica?"

"Mom? Where are you? Why aren't you at work? I tried you just this—"

"Erica, I have to see Simon Fleming."

"What a coincidence, he's trying a case for us right now. I got on to him and he said he would take it, heaven bless him, so he's—"

"I know. I just wanted to find out what courtroom."

Silence. She could hear Erica tell someone to hang on, be there in a minute. Then, "Mom, you're not in trouble, are you?"

"I haven't been raped, if that's what you mean. But there are, um, complications."

"Oh, Lord, it's David, isn't it? When you use that tone of voice, always David. Mom darling, if you didn't have to carry that all alone."

She murmured something—no problem—but even as she heard her deprecating words, she knew Erica was right. She does have it alone. What she told Ken about David's turning off his friends is half the story; the other half is that because she refuses to be turned off, withstands every rebuff, makes clear that a thick skin is her chosen response to his touchy pride, she is indeed on her own. Her baby.

"Mom? Want me to go down with you? I'd thought of going anyhow, I just got so jammed up here. Wait a sec." Another aside to someone: she would call right back.

Oh, does she ever want Erica to come with her. That tall, lovely girl, all sweetness and masterful efficiency, on whose competent shoulders she can unload her burden. Erica darling, your Uncle David is fixing to kill Sandy Fleming, and I'm not sure how to handle it.

She looked out at the woman who was waiting with ostentatious patience to use the phone and said of course not, she just wanted to make sure where she was headed, she's at a subway entrance right now, she can make her own way down to Center Street.

"It's nothing serious, is it? This problem of David's?"

A laugh that resounds against the Plexiglas walls. Serious? Not really. Except insofar as everything to do with him takes on a certain seriousness.

"Well, look, I've been remiss. No, it's true, don't say it. I'll meet you there for Sunday brunch, okay?"

"Sounds good." She put the receiver to her other ear, to shut out the sight of that purposeful face beyond the glass. "This Simon Fleming. What does he look like?"

"Imposing. Suntanned. Hair worn in longish little-boy cut, but don't let that fool you, he's a dynamo under that wholesome charm. Mom, one-thirty now, if you hurry you just might catch him before they start again after lunch."

She did hurry but she didn't catch him; afternoon session was just starting when she made her way to a seat in the fourth row. Imposing, suntanned, longish hair, Erica had said—enough to single out the man who stood up from the counsel's table and, after the woman on the witness stand had taken her oath, started leading her through the events of an evening eight months earlier. He led her without expression: the dynamo as deadpan guide. There were no dramatics, no oratorical flourishes; from his position against the low barrier, he didn't even move except at one point to return to the table to take a piece of paper from a briefcase. And he made no special effort to coddle or indulge his witness. In a flat tone, like a teacher ascertaining whether some pupil has done the assignments, he put the questions. Miss Florio, do you remember the evening of September 18th? Can you tell the jury what happened? Where was he standing when you took out your keys? In what hand was he holding the knife? Do you recognize this picture, Miss Florio?

And the woman responded in kind. Though her face when she started was set in a taut smile, almost an unseemly smile, gradually a constrained gravity took over. She sat straight; she looked from time to time, as no doubt advised, at the jurors; she kept her hands folded in her lap. She was someone following but also declaiming, taking her cues from his sturdy matter-of-factness. And responding in a voice that was softer than his but matched it in clarity. Yes, she had met the defendant that night at a party. Yes, she got voluntarily into the taxi with him. No, she did not invite him into her apartment. No, she did not unlock her door until he pulled out the knife. Yes, she struggled, she tried to get to the phone—a quick, defiant, challenging look at his point at the defendant. Well, yes, he was holding the knife when she walked ahead of him into the bedroom . . . in a voice the jurors could hear, even Margaret in the fourth row could hear, the woman answered, so when Simon Fleming worked up at last to the crucial question with his high-voltage words—penis, vagina, penetrate—her voice was steady as she made the damning assertion. By now she was crying; her voice trembled; she reached out to the cup of water beside her, but, a triumph, she made the assertion. Margaret met the gaze of the woman beside her, and they both sighed. Done and done: some force extending from the motionless man to the woman some fifteen feet away had got her through. He was supporting her without extending visible support. Holding her up without implying there might be anything to pull her down. Affording her the chance to exploit the crime without appearing to denigrate her person. His didactic voice went out, and it was as if he said, You're okay, just hold on, I'm with you.

The attorney for the defendant was not with her. Though his tone began as ingratiating, though he introduced himself with excessive courtesy and moved with pointed informality around the room, implicit in his questions was a different message. You invited him in, you wanted it, you asked for it, there was no rape. Different message and different response. She broke down. She sobbed. She contradicted herself. She spoke so softly the stenographer had to ask to have that repeated, please. She said she didn't remember, so it took two recesses and two talks at the bench before the judge finally said the jury was excused, the case would continue at ten the next morning.

Margaret leaned over the barrier. "Mr. Fleming? I'm Margaret Berringer. David Bynam's sister. Erica Berringer's mother. I wonder if we could talk for a few minutes." It was urgent, she added to his look of mild dubiety.

He took a second to size her up; those cool gray eyes, she thought, had done plenty of sizing up. "Well, sure. Good to meet you, Mrs. Berringer. I'll just get my papers together and say good-bye to some of these people—won't be five minutes."

It was ten minutes, then he joined her at the door. Would she like to come up to his office? Or if she's rushed, someplace around here? There's a coffee shop around the corner.

Coffee shop; when they stood waiting for the elevator, she said he'd been wonderful.

He brushed it off. "Any lawyer."

"Any lawyer wouldn't handle that woman the way you did. Keeping her calm and combative both."

He walked beside her through the crowded hall and said the real point was, any lawyer wouldn't take the case because he wouldn't have Erica egging him on. "There was a case in that same courtroom just last week. Same judge, same alleged offense. End of sameness. That one had all the staples. Strange intruder breaking in, mother and eighteen-year-old daughter trapped together, hands and feet tied to bedposts, pillowcases over heads—the works. And the worst of it, the part that doesn't bear thinking about, the mother told if she doesn't resist, he will leave the daughter alone. After which—you guessed it—the girl's turn . . . the kind of case the D.A.'s office jumps at. Big glory and no risks. But this one—well, you heard. The woman probably flirted with him at the party. She was glad to get into a taxi with him. Maybe she let him kiss her. She's no young innocent—all things for the defense attorney to make hay of. Tomorrow he'll start making hay with a vengeance. I happen to believe that woman's story, but can we make the jury believe it? Maybe not. With all the calm veracity from that witness, maybe not. I know it, she knows it, your daughter knew it when she got me into it. Well, here's the place. Let's hope they have an empty table."

A small table in back. He sat, leaned his head on his hands, and said, "Now, Mrs. Berringer, what can I do for you?"

Her third go at this in one day: she ought to have it down pat. My brother David; your brother Sandy. Plus the tatters of that desperate excuse: swimming pool . . . circulatory system . . . maybe . . . what if.

Simon Fleming was amenable. Not like the other two. Myra had relegated David to a stereotype marked Invalid and offered suggestions for him in that capacity, and Kenneth Ash had viewed the pool as an engineering challenge and shown how something called the vertical load could be managed. None of that for this man. Sitting on the wire chair that was too small for his impressive frame, he made clear where his interest lay.

He himself would like to invest money, was what he said. If this enterprise was something worthwhile, if there was a one in a hundred chance that it would turn out worthwhile, count on him to pitch in. He knew how Sandy felt about David Bynam: that overwhelming desire to help. As Sandy's brother, he inevitably felt a portion of that pressure. Any contribution he could make would be a favor to him.

She told the waitress just coffee please. "It's really good of you."

"In fact—I always wanted the chance to say this—I'd very much like to assist your brother in any way. After all, the exorbitant cost of the care someone in his circumstances must need."

She smiled and said no thank you. "He has enough for everything. For nurses and equipment and a special car and for running a lavish house and also for travel if he wanted but he doesn't want. He was a rich man when it happened. Actually, he was rich at thirty. Boy wonder. And then with all that insurance."

"So what we now need is for Sandy to certify this possibly constructive setup."

She nodded.

He leaned forward on the small table. Perhaps this question was out of order, but he couldn't help wondering. Sandy had a wife and partner. How come she didn't—

"I did go to them. First Myra, then Ken Ash. They couldn't be sure which hotel or even which job. But Ken said he'd heard Sandy say he would call you from the trip, so we thought maybe—"

Simon waited a minute. A man at the next table gave a gratified nod, and she recognized him as having sat two rows ahead of her at the trial. "Mrs. Berringer, am I right in the assumption that if you've gone to all this trouble to contact Sandy in Chicago, this matter is really important to you?"

She said yes. Really important.

"Am I further right in assuming that it concerns some psychological involvement between your brother and Sandy that it's not necessary for the two of us to examine closely?"

She said that was exactly right.

"And can I further assume that if I tell you that the promised phone call from Sandy to me may not materialize, I won't sound like your other two unavailing communicants?"

He's treating me like a witness. Well, it's a technique he's good at. She said with a sigh she supposed so.

Above the clatter from the restaurant, his formidable voice went smoothly on. He had a client who ran a small chain of hotels. If he pulled the appropriate strings and drew on past favors, he thought they might well be able to find out whether a Sanford Fleming was registered at a Chicago hotel.

He waved away the waitress. "Of course there's always the possibility that he'll have stayed at the home of a friend. Plenty of friends, I expect, would jump at the chance to have him. But I know my brother. Along with the easy-going charm there are some fastidious standards. He's not the kind to put up with the inferior mattress or the inadequate lighting or the mismatched furniture of someone's guest room. For him, it'll be a hotel, and if my hunch is correct, an exemplary one."

She studied the impressive face under the deftly cut hair. How eminently sensible. How judicious: pragmatism coinciding with psychology to get her what she wants. "You make it sound so easy."

Way a favor ought to sound, he said.

She put down her cup; any more coffee and she will float away. "That phone call from Sandy to you. Ken told me you're in the running for a nomination for congressman?"

"It's no secret. Anyone who knows me has had to put up with it this past year. Poor Sandy, he's put up with it most of all—I guess that's what brothers are for." He offered his curtailed smile. "If you were in my district, would you vote for me?"

She gave an honest nod. She'd vote for him, the waitress who kept hovering to see if they wanted anything else would, those he had mesmerized on the jury would, his compliant client would, the man at the next table who kept throwing furtive looks in his direction would. His speech might be a little too loaded with oracular pronouncements, what Erica called the little-boy style of his hair might be too studied, but they'd know, these putative constituents, here was someone who could handle things; their interest would be in good hands. They'd vote for him, they'd keep on voting, year after year.

"I hope you get the nomination. If you really want it, that is."

"You don't tie yourself in the knots and make the promises and engage in the manipulations necessary to get this far if you don't want it," he said with the practiced candor that would be another asset. "Are you really asking? I want it, my wife is good enough to say she wants it, my two young sons are deluded enough to think they want it."

"Model family."

"What we're counting on," he said.

She looked into her empty cup. "You'd surely have my vote," she said again. Because how not vote for one who handles you like a valued constituent: gives attention to your problem, goes easy with the questions, refrains from making judgments, comes up with a solution? The buck stops here.

FIVE

IT WAS RAINING when she got to David's apartment the next afternoon, and in her soaked shoes, she paused at the door. In her own apartment she would slosh right in. Here it's important to make a stand for spotless rugs and shining floors, to show that appearance *counts*—in her stockinged feet, she walked over to the wheelchair.

"Hi, darling. How's everything?"

"I think the cough is getting worse."

She bent to kiss him. Standard: if there's trouble, let her in on it right away.

"I think I'm not propped high enough when I sleep. Maybe it's the bed. I told Lawrence we should have them come and look at it." He gave a small demonstrative cough. "See what I mean?"

What she saw was that if it weren't this minor irritation, it would be something else. The inventory of his health problems constituted for him the saga of his life. Barred by rancor, by perverse pride, from looking out, he looked within—literally within. To lungs, heart, stomach, kidney, colon. He paid an overwrought attention to the workings of these organs, panicked over the possibilities of damage, was on the continual lookout for signs of gallstones, infection, bedsores, cardiac trouble, pneumonia. At the same time, he sometimes went into depressions so black that he seriously contemplated suicide. At least twice, an alert attendant had found the place where he was secreting sleeping pills, and once she had seen him through a bout of noneating that brought him to the edge of dehydration. I'm not good for anything, why don't I just kill myself—juxtaposed almost in the same breath with, That new medicine isn't right, I have to call the doctor.

"Maggie, love, I'm a pill, you must hate me."

"Don't be a simp." She sat opposite him.

He flashed his brotherly smile. How was her day?

Her day had been not hearing from Sandy. Well, she could hardly expect to. Even with all systems working, that hotel chain couldn't produce results so fast. And there was time. Tuesday now—not coming home till Saturday, they had said.

She said her day was busy—her secretary out sick but nothing serious—and how about his?

"Nothing much going on. I read. Listened to some records. Went through some circulars. The dull usual."

She looked around the room in which this dull usual took place. A room that proclaimed what could be done to alleviate impairment: stairs replaced by a ramp that a wheelchair could navigate, doors widened so a wheelchair could get through, shelves rebuilt so an arm in a wheelchair could comfortably reach in, the small beautiful rugs discarded lest a wheelchair disastrously slip, light switches and door handles lowered—all the conveniences money and expertise could provide.

The door to the kitchen was opening now. "Smells good. What's for dinner?"

"Veal chops." Lawrence came in carrying a tray with pills and a glass of water. "Stuffed veal chops with prosciutto, the way Mr. Bynam likes them. I just hope he eats them."

Made the way Lawrence likes them, she amended silently. When he bent to put down the tray, she noticed the bulging waist under his white coat. They all gained weight in David's service, ordering the choicest provisions for him and partaking of a good share of it themselves. "Stuffed veal chops," she said. "Who wouldn't eat them?"

"He had a hot dog." Lawrence spoke with the jokingly censorious tone suitable for invalids or small children.

"Can't kid me, Mr. Bynam. I saw the wrapping paper in the bottom of the car when you brought it back. That stand on Long Island you always say is so great."

She waited till Lawrence went out. "The dull usual, you said."

"Drive on a wet spring day. That's usual, isn't it?" He fingered a pill but didn't take it.

"You went to the house?"

"Maggie, love, the car is set to go there. Automatic pilot."

She sat stiffly. Sandy not due back till Saturday. Besides, you always hear if anything happens. It was what she used to tell herself in the days when Erica was in the stage of going out with boys who drove too fast, drank too much. You always hear. Except when you don't.

"Anyone around out there?" her tight voice asked.

David shook his head vaguely and picked up the pills—this time he did swallow them, a single proficient gulp. "Funny. When the accident happened I couldn't swallow pills. It was just a knack I didn't have, had never felt any inclination to cultivate. No pills, I told the doctor, I can't handle them. Ha! Who would think that six times daily, what am I talking about, eight times a day, step up, ladies and gentlemen, watch David the trained seal swallow his—"

He's stalling. Is it because he has a reason to stall? "David, tell me about the trip."

"Maggie, relax. Nothing to tell. Trees starting to bud, grass turning, those yellow what's-their-name flowers along the road. Uneventful."

Uneventful, but the fact remains that he would not have mentioned it unless Lawrence had forced his hand. "Talk to anyone?"

"I did, as a matter of fact. I stopped at the farm stand on the way out. Remember it? Nice little place just where the road forks off. Nothing to buy, too early, but the fellow had plenty to say about real estate. Skyrocketing out there even worse than the city. There was a lot right next door to him, not even a water view and so narrow they had to get a variance to build, it tripled in price in just the past two years. And this other lot, just a few yards from that new rec center, noisy every night but still..." Hearty, authoritative, his voice went on: deals, mortgages, increments, variances, profits. This was what interested him: not the budding trees but the skyrocketing real estate.

It was also what would interest Simon, she suddenly thought. The Simon whose idea of providing assistance was to offer money. They were similar, the man with the tanned, impressive, well-groomed head and her brother in his wheelchair. Two forthright, purposeful men. Geared for success, intolerant of bad luck—bad luck was for some other people. If Simon Fleming had been injured by a man's negligence, he also might feel the urge to seek vengeance with a gun.

"Hey, Maggie, are you really upset?"

"You know I am."

"Suppose I tell you I won't go out there again. That make you feel better?"

She turned to him. Is he being perverse? Or going through the motions of humoring her? Her gaze went over him: glen plaid trousers, silk shirt, cashmere vest, suede shoes. Another perversity: he turned off overtures of friendship, invented obstacles for would-be visitors, said, No, um, next Thursday won't be a good time, but sitting alone day after day he was set for company, a man dressed to the teeth.

"David, don't kid about this."

"I'm not. I promise. No more trips out there." It just might be true: the sardonic look had given way to one of deep sobriety. "That part of Long Island won't see me again, I swear it."

She was suddenly lighthearted. He means it. He wouldn't say it if he didn't mean it. Her breath went out in such a long sigh that he was the one scrutinizing her.

"Maggie, you look tired."

"Big report due at the office," she murmured.

He put his head judicially to one side. "Don't come tomorrow. I want you to buy yourself some new clothes— Maggie, don't make a face, it's on me—and get your hair done and your skin and whatever else they do in those places. Soup to nuts. You hear? My beautiful sister has to take care of her beauty."

Pure affection looked out of the blue eyes. It's a serious proposition. He will make the sacrifice of giving up her company. And it is a sacrifice. Her daily visit brings the world with it: his link to sanity. Paid help can't provide this, the most efficient and intelligent and compassionate of nurses can't provide it. By treating his invalidism, they gradually partake of it, come under its stealthy dominance. But by being of his household and also not of it, she gives him his hold on normalcy, and in his moments of disinterested reasonableness, he knows it.

"Maggie, want a drink? I think Lawrence fixed us some little goodies. Lawrence? Oh, Lawrence, thanks, what we wanted. And listen to this. Mrs. Berringer isn't coming tomorrow, we can get on without her, can't we? Sure, what I told her."

Two pairs of eyes brimming with their courteous injunction. Lawrence bowed: the discreet gesture of one who senses complications and knows he should distance himself from them. At the same time, she suddenly wondered, how much does he know? They live in such intimacy, David and whoever takes care of him—how can there possibly be secrets? Does Lawrence understand, for instance, what barely suppressed goal takes David out to the site where he had his accident? Did he let fall that information about the hot dog wrapper with full cognizance of its import for an anxious sister. Did he discern, as that sister stood there in her businesswoman's suit and her stockinged feet, that her blood was running cold?

Oh, this is crazy. David is right, she needs time off. Especially after those strained conversations yesterday, she needs it. Usually, at this point in her visit, she wanders into the kitchen: peers into pantry shelves, runs a hand over Formica counters, opens the refrigerator to see that the fruit is fresh and the salad dressing made the way David likes it. Again a big difference from her own apartment, where the ficus can die of neglect, the venetian blinds can accumulate dust, bits of leftover cheese can turn blue, and it's no big deal. But in a setup like this, where the patient endures total dependence and the custodian enjoys tempting autonomy, you have to keep up standards. Whoever is in charge has to know that someone else is in super charge: Big Sister is watching you.

She'd skip all that today. The hour from five-thirty to six-thirty tomorrow free for whatever she wanted—she felt detached already. When the doorbell rang, she paid no attention: let Lawrence handle it, as tomorrow he would handle everything. So it wasn't until the policemen were positioned on either side of the wheelchair, wearing the smiles of diffident unease that David always inspired in anyone seeing him for the first time, that she realized detachment at this particular time was not in the cards.

SIX

THEY TREATED HIM with decorous gravity at the police station. Indeed, once the policemen had got over their shock at being confronted by someone in David's condition, they treated him with decorous gravity before he even went to the police station. Because they assured him it was not essential that he come to the station at all, there were some questions to ask him in regard to the death of Sandy Fleming, but it could be arranged that someone interview him here at home.

Death: that was what she heard. Death by what means? In what place? In deference to a man who was a paraplegic, could murder be subsumed under the euphemism of "death"?

David, however, heard something else. Could be arranged. He heard the phrase, heard in some sensitive part of his mind the subtly patronizing note, and his brows lowered over the intensely blue eyes. What was the established procedure in cases like this? One went to the precinct? Very well, he would go. No, it was not too much trouble, if they would excuse him he would be ready in a few minutes.

Of course it was trouble. Any break in the routine was trouble. Any circumstance that had him leaving his meticulously regulated environment was trouble. And particular trouble leaving at six-thirty, which was the hour when the other men in the building came home, tossing their offhand greetings to the doorman and strolling with briefcases and newspapers and expressions of justified fatigue across the lobby. He tried to avoid this hour. She knew he did everything so as not to expose himself to the heavy friendliness inevitable at this hour. But now, being pushed in his wheelchair, he had to face those prototypes of his old self, face them, indeed, along with a pair of policemen who for all their tactfulness could not make themselves invisible.

So the police station was a kind of relief. At a police station people don't stop to gaze at a man in a wheelchair. Too much else is going on. Too many other people with problems are being ushered in or out. Too much drama is being played out in front of the high desk. Without undue fuss, the policemen waited while Lawrence lifted David out of the car, and then, taking over the wheelchair, they escorted him to Detective Moss, who said if Mr. Bynam would prefer, his sister could stay with him during the questioning. No? That would not be necessary? In that case, Mrs. Berringer, would you wait in here?

Here was an office just big enough to hold a desk and a couple of chairs. She looked around, at the faded green walls, the stained floor, the papers piled in one corner, and thought of all the stories she'd ever heard of police brutality. They push people around. They aim 300-watt lights at the subject's eyes. They alternate ingratiating tones and sadistic ones. Out of range of the camera, they slap faces and punch stomachs: Now, will you admit that you did it?

Except in David's case the brutality would be tailored to him. Canny tacticians that they were, they would catch on fast to what threw him. Go easy, the guy's a cripple, one of them would mutter. Better let the poor slob take a rest, his sidekick would agree. Only half a man, give him a break, some sanctimonious voice would suggest. Until goaded, furious, strangled by his feverish pride, he would blurt out what they wanted to hear.

Well, what is it they want? A dependable culprit for the crime, of course. Because there has been a crime: Sandy Fleming murdered on that site on Long Island—the one fact the police would divulge on that laconic ride from David's apartment. That and the time: between twelve and one this afternoon.

One o'clock: she had been in her office, going over data to ascertain whether a small-town newspaper would be well-advised to add a homemaking section to its Friday edition. She had sent investigators to Ohio last week to ask the pertinent questions—Do you ever read menus in the newspaper? What part of the paper do you read first? How much time daily do you spend in the kitchen?—and for a whole afternoon she had sat, the busy innocent, collating, tabulating, correlating. See, you don't always hear, after all.

"Ma'am, would you like some coffee?" A policeman from the adjoining room—past him she could see a handcuffed man in a chair. Would they put handcuffs on someone whose arms were his only usable limbs?

"Oh, no. No, thank you." Stupid. She wants coffee, is longing for it. It is being here she doesn't want, appropriated into this process, someone programmed in for their wary talk and ritual sympathy.

But she is here, she and David, along with the tape machines, the videos, the handcuffs, the expedient brutality—the two of them are what the process is all about. They are here although less than an hour ago David turned to her his gaze of stolid melancholy and said, Oh, nothing much, just the dull usual for the afternoon. Lawrence caught that one, but what other untruths were encompassed by his bleak recital? Okay, communication between them has hit a staggering low. She went to the door and then sat again, and to stop the inner pounding, she turned her mind back, back to more felicitous exchanges she and David had had over the years. Before his valedictory speech on graduating from high school: "Swear you'll sit in the front row, Mag, otherwise I know I'll crack up." When she left home to go to college: "Be dullsville around here without you, kid." When he was thinking of getting married: "She reminds me of you, Mag, so I think I'll chance it." When the firm made him a partner: "Maggie, remember all the times you did my arithmetic homework for me?"

And the time he called and said, "Maggie, there's this guy I play golf with, I told him about my gorgeous sister, if he calls for a drink next week, do me a favor and say yes." She said lots of yesses after that. She was wholly inclined to say yes. This guy turned out to be bright, successful, insensitive, and a pleasure to go to bed with—when she was twenty-two, it filled the bill. His business was a factory that made some small but indispensable part for machines, which in turn made of its balance sheet a barometer of the country's economic weather. If Alex came in depressed of an evening, she would know that next day on the financial page there would be dire forecasts, vice presidents resigning, bank closings, arcane graphs headed down. If on the other hand he said, Go buy yourself a fur coat, it was a sign to watch for rosy outlooks, bullish stock market, housing starts going up. It gave her a feeling of being at the heart of things. Alex and Margaret: where the action was.

And he and David remained friends. That was a fact of the marriage: Alex indoctrinated by David into the joys of yachting, David induced by Alex to get over his disinclination for the cold so they could whiz down ski trails together. Her husband and her brother: it satisfied some need within her for harmonious arrangements. It also gave her strength, so when Alex had his fling with the efficiency expert, it was David who explained that when a man hit a certain age...no repetition of the incident...the lure of business intimacy...all the bromides she took to heart because it was her brother offering them.

"I can go home." The wheelchair was at the door.

"I should hope so."

"If they're not satisfied, they can keep you." He spoke airily, as if keeping him would entail no special complications.

All right, if that's how he wants to play it. "I suppose they can."

"It was an interesting session," he said.

"Glad to hear it."

"The detectives seemed not unintelligent."

Is he going to keep it up all the way home, the flip chatter of one who has spent the evening at some mildly amusing entertainment? He didn't feel flip; she saw the pallor of his face, the way his hands gripped the armrests and his shoulders tightened as Lawrence pushed him across the parking lot, so the business of lifting from chair to car was harder than usual. But he quieted as soon as they started driving, and then nothing till they pulled up in front of his apartment.

"Maggie, you go on home now." His prosaic, everyday voice.

"Don't be dumb."

"True. I don't need you."

"David, shut up."

"You must be starved. And nothing to eat up there— Lawrence, isn't it a fact?—except a chop apiece."

"I'm coming up, idiot."

A long look from those guarded eyes. But the maneuvers were starting again: slide, lift, carry, slide, push, greeting to well-meaning neighbors—yes, fine weather, fine thanks, yes—the process that took all his patience, all his concentration, all his disciplined control until he was beside the window of the living room and she was in the comfortable chair opposite.

Then at least no more flippancy. He looked at the closed door to the kitchen, arranged his hands on the armrests, and told her what the police had told him. Sandy had been shot. He was found in front of the house, or what there was of the house. He had been lying there, it was thought, less than half an hour before someone came by to deliver lumber. "Or was it bricks? Now I think of it, they did say bricks.

Though I can't imagine why bricks, there's no place in that construction where—"

"David, go *on*."

"That's all. They found him. They called an ambulance but no use. He was dead." Still the flat voice, the strained hands.

Well, not quite all. "David, what about you?"

"Me!" he said in a tone of ironic surprise. "I didn't kill him."

"I know you didn't." But he must have heard the tremor in her voice. They sat looking at each other, the adversarial stare of people who have not yet put their defenses in order.

"Maggie, didn't you have a dinner date?"

"David, quit it."

"I'm sorry I loused up your evening."

He can't help doing this, taunting her, holding her off; it's one of the few exercises of power available to him.

"Okay, teacher. You want the whole story? Well, then, the truth is I did see Sandy. I didn't kill him but I saw him."

"Ah."

"I told the police. I decided that was best. They knew the time he landed at the airport; for all I knew they could also check the time I left my garage; maybe they'd even get to that man at the fruit stand. You know, the one I talked to. So I figured if they were going to find out anyhow..."

They're not even moving along the same track. All that saga of closeness in the past, but a calculating stranger sits opposite her. She wants facts, is frantic for them, and the stranger goes on about tactics: Will candor serve better than duplicity, are they bound to catch on anyhow, what course will prove most expedient?

"David, what else?"

"It was raining, you know that. The road's not so good after the rain, some bad bumps once you pass the farm stand but no mishap for this daring driver. I was thinking about Sandy, naturally I was—who am I kidding, I don't drive out there for the scenery. So he's on my mind, and when I get to the house, damned if his car isn't there. Nifty Italian model. Unmistakable.'' His voice, with its slight mocking note, wound down. "Sure you want to hear all this? You don't have to.''

She folded her hands.

"Okay. More details. So Sandy must have heard the noise even though he was on the other side of the house or let's say what there is of the house. The water side. Right away he starts walking up. He's wearing one of those long bulky sweaters he goes in for, very sporty.'' David looked for a second at his own sport clothes. An outfit for the visitors who are not allowed to visit. "Don't ask me who he thought it was. Some workman, maybe. Someone he was meeting in a car he didn't know. Anyhow, he had to watch his step, holes in the ground from all that rain, boards lying around, bags of cement, what not. What I mean is, there was a whole minute when I could have done it.'' The door opened: Lawrence with a glass of fruit juice which he set with a dictatorial nod on the wheelchair tray. David waited for the door to close. "Where was I? Yes. An easy shot. While he was watching out for a loose plank. When he had to circle a mound of dirt and stone. When he made his way over those flagstones they laid down where the ground was soft. A cinch. Raise my gun, aim, fire. But—Maggie, don't look like that. I told you I didn't. Okay?''

"Okay.'' Her lips made no sound.

"So why didn't I shoot him? Maggie, love, I suppose you want me to say because I knew it would be wrong, I couldn't bring myself to do something so out of character.'' Light from the standing lamp shone on his broad, handsome, sardonic face.

Yes. Exactly what she does want.

"Morality. Inner goodness. Forget all that rot.'' He turned the wheelchair a few inches. "I didn't because I decided he would suffer more if I left him alive. Shooting—a second and it's over. Instant death—this was my thinking, anyhow—too good for that bastard. I wanted him always to have that prospect of me with the gun on him, so he'd never know when I—''

"You mean he saw you!"

"How could he not, once he got close enough? What else would he be looking at?''

"David, you—Oh, Lawrence, nothing to eat now, please just leave us a second. You say you and Sandy—tell me again.'' But she doesn't need it again; this is what she will always hold in mind: not Sandy dead, that undefined image relayed at third hand by a police officer, but Sandy making his way across the jumbled mess of a construction job, the smile of welcome freezing on his round mild face, while a few feet away a man leans out of his car, his gaze steely, his lips set above the bent elbow and ready hand. What did Sandy say, she asked.

"Nothing. He said nothing, I said nothing. I just sat there, gun in hand, and the idea hit me. If I don't shoot he'll shiver in his pants the rest of his life. Each time he crosses a quiet street. Whenever he walks alone at night. Any morning he wakes up and looks at the sky and thinks maybe today the cripple will get him . . . Maggie, you all right?''

"I suppose so.''

"Cheer up, lovey. I didn't tell this part to the police. About my holding a gun on him.''

"I see.''

"Under the circumstances, I decided to say I had a gun but I kept it the whole time in my pocket and threw it away on the way home.''

"Good thinking.''

"I figured, not knowing all the background, they might misunderstand my motives.''

She said she could see how they well might.

David gulped down the fruit juice: a man performing his assigned function. "I didn't tell them why I threw the gun away either," he said.

"What's that?"

"The gun, I don't have it anymore. Maggie, you look tired, sure you want to hear?"

She doesn't want to. She feels a sudden revulsion against hearing. Why must she be part of it, this misbegotten project that one way or other has ended in tragedy? She said sure she wanted to and he told her, the sordid facts doled out in his voice of whimsical callousness. What he did was throw the gun into some water on the way home. One of those streams or bays or inlets—no, he didn't notice the exact location, so many of them along the route. He waited until he was roughly in the middle of a small bridge, and no other car seemed to be around, and he tossed. Good-bye gun. Not even a splash, or rather there probably was but impossible to hear when one is driving.

"Why did I do it? That what you're wondering? I figured, suppose Sandy made a fuss and went crying to the police about how I was trying to kill him—not likely but to my mind a possibility—anyhow, if he went, and they came here to check up, not so helpful if under my sport shirts they found a small blue Beretta. Ironic, Maggie, isn't it? Because now if I had that gun I could show them it was never fired."

That's not the only irony. She sat motionless.

"But as I say, that's between you and me. The police think I threw it away because I no longer wanted to have it."

"What else do they think?"

He gave her a quick look, but his tone continued placid. "To tell the truth, they seemed more interested in my car than anything else. A car with manual controls—fascinating. Where did I get it and how did it work and what kind of repair bills? One of the detectives had a disabled cousin, or did he say uncle, anyhow, the fellow's been thinking about a car like that, he could really use one, but when I told them the price..."

Procrastinating again. Well, why shouldn't he procrastinate?

"So, Maggie, that's it. I gave them the whole story. Sandy was there, we saw each other, but I didn't shoot him. God, no. I just nodded and he nodded back and I drove away. I didn't pretend the visit was an exercise in belated friendliness, but I didn't describe any hostility either, why the hell should I?"

Right, why should he? But the fact remains that he didn't tell them the whole story. He didn't tell them about other trips he had made out there to check up on Sandy, or about waiting for hours in front of home and office in order to see what Sandy was up to, or about his blazing need to kill Sandy, naturally he didn't tell them any of that. Also—she stared out the window—he didn't tell them that just two hours ago, sitting here, he had assured his sister he would not go out to that site again, the project was finished—that promise so susceptible of a dual interpretation was missing from his account.

"So they are satisfied?" she fatuously asked.

"Must have been." His tone matched hers: showy complacence. "After all, they did say I could go on home."

That doesn't exactly mean they were satisfied. She sat looking at the view. Block after block of lights, towers, scaffolding, windows, interesting juxtapositions of forms and space. A view to intrigue an invalid, who usually kept his chair turned slightly away from it.

The chair was turned now. "He was not a bad guy," David said, and didn't have to tell her of whom he was talking.

"Uh huh."

"Careless, inexcusably negligent, probably not endowed with some talents even a mediocre architect is supposed to possess, but not intrinsically bad."

She lowered her head. It's Sandy Fleming's eulogy, courtesy David Bynam. One is not inclined to deliver that kind of eulogy about a man one has killed. One is inclined to deliver that kind of eulogy about a man one has killed. Which?

"And he had some indisputable virtues. All that easygoing charm, that ability to sell you on a design with just a wave of his fingers—after all, with the field wide open, he's the one I chose to build the house."

She gave a neutral nod.

"He didn't strike me as the kind to have enemies," David said.

"Except you," she could not stop herself from saying.

"Right. Except me."

Another portentous silence. Dark in here, she noted. Does the lamp in the corner always do such an inefficient job? She must get a better lamp, or at least put stronger bulbs into the one that is there.

David looked at her across the room. "Hey, Maggie, you believe me, don't you? I didn't do it. Not guilty."

Well, there it is. The question that's been hanging over them all evening, that he didn't have to ask because both of them had been inescapably fixed on it. While he was parrying the awkward solicitations of his neighbors, or maintaining a purposeful silence against Lawrence's well-trained impassivity, or reacting with staged flippancy to the discomfort of official inquiry, or even assembling for her the implausible details of his aborted visit, the question was there. Does she believe him?

Okay, the answer is, she does. Though he did his best to mislead her earlier, still the only possible answer. The only one commensurate with people murmuring, "Twins? Cute" when they were growing up together, and with her required presence in the front row while he made his valedictory speech, and with his choosing a girl to marry because of her sisterly resemblance, and with her obligation today to make sure his kitchen is stocked with his favorite foods. He's my brother, of course I believe him. Unlikely as it sounds, his story about not having shot Sandy is true.

But what he doesn't know, she thought, seeing the assertive nod of her head reflected in the assured lift of his shoulders, what he must never know, is that she is involved. She got in on it, a gratuitous and, as it turned out, fruitless exposure. She interjected herself into a circumstance that, with massive reverberations, has now moved out from under her control.

SEVEN

SUN WAS POURING into David's living room when she arrived next morning. "Good morning, darling. Oh, hello, Lawrence, going out just when I come in?"

"He has to take some things to the tailor," David said, "but I wanted him to wait for you in case our friends the police show up again." He nodded to Lawrence, who had two pairs of trousers over his arm. So now did they have it straight? Two inches shorter for the blue ones, one and half, with cuffs, for the tan—was that what they had agreed?

Lawrence checked a piece of paper. That was it, he said, and bowed, an even more portly figure in his own jacket than encased in the white coat. She waited until she heard the elevator.

"David, what was that all about?"

"This store where I've been buying slacks for twenty years, you'd think they'd have my measurements by now, but this time what they sent—"

"David, please."

"I wanted to talk to you in private." He allowed a sullen smile.

"That was very obvious. Darling, isn't it a little late to try to shield Lawrence from the facts of—"

"This is facts about Lawrence." He maneuvered his wheelchair away from the window. "I want to talk about *him*."

"Ah."

"Maggie, that business yesterday, didn't something seem odd when you thought it over?"

"Well, David, of course. My God, for them to think that you—"

"I mean, the timing. Look what happens. Sandy is shot between twelve and one. At six o'clock, just five hours later, they have a case against me. Complete with details about car, garage, route, conversations with local characters, transaction at hot dog stand . . . the kind of details they'd work up only if they got started on it immediately. If someone, that is, made a definite pronouncement—David Bynam is your man—as soon as they heard about the murder. Maggie, think about it."

She had thought. At midnight, when she turned off her light, and at two, when she took the first sleeping pill, and again at six, when she lay in bed and thought, Quiet, heart, you just don't know, it could have happened that way even without your interference.

"Of course I'd expect them to get around to me eventually. Just a matter of tossing out the standard question: Can you think of anyone who felt hostility, et cetera. But on the kind of vague suspicion that inspires they don't jump right in, send their operatives scurrying around to East Side garages and Long Island fruit stands."

"David, what are you trying to say?"

"Lawrence," his portentous voice said. "My man Lawrence."

She studied the view. A different city by day, sun and shadows making wholly new configurations of those rearing towers. "He was here with us when the police came, none of us knew the first thing—"

"You and I didn't know because we don't listen to local news broadcasts. But Lawrence goes out for his free hour sometimes between one and three—yesterday he went early, before one. So let's say he stopped at some bar where they have TV, and he heard the news—Sandy Fleming found shot—and then he picked up the phone. The unsolicited tip the police will give their eye teeth for."

"Where would he get the idea that you . . ."

"By listening to you and me talk, that's where. Oh, I know, we keep up the fiction that by closing doors we maintain secrecy. But check it out, Maggie. Go in the kitchen right now and close the door and I'll say something in my natural voice, and you'll see how—"

"No," she said loudly. "No!"

"Besides, look how he told you about that hot dog. That wasn't any casual remark, he knew exactly what he was doing."

It was on the tip of her tongue to say, if you hadn't tried to mislead me, he would not have had that chance to correct you. She turned away. Another side effect of this whole business: she can no longer get angry at him, the cavalier explosion into honest indignation has been ruled out.

"A call to the police—why in the world would he do it?"

David steered himself across the room. "Maybe there's good money in information like that. No? You don't think so? Maybe he did it just for the heck of it. Maybe he was miffed because I criticized the way my shirts were hanging yesterday. Maybe some cockeyed idea of glory. Or, I don't know, Maggie, maybe deep down, at some level he doesn't recognize himself, he really does hate me. God knows I feel silent rage often enough, maybe it also goes the other way; someone in his position resents the man whom necessity forces him to bathe and feed and dress and indulge in small talk sixteen hours a day."

She saw his twisted face, and for a second the idea fluttered. Why shouldn't I tell him? A man capable of such discernment about his own situation would surely understand a sister's compulsion. David, I have to tell you—I tried to warn Sandy. As it turned out, I saw his wife, his partner, and his brother. I didn't want you to do something you would forever regret. I put it obliquely, of course, me and my cagey excuses, but it's just possible that after Sandy was killed one of them saw through my story. In which case that person might have been the one to inform the police.... It would clear the air. Not just exonerate Lawrence but put David and her on the kind of forthright footing she longs for.

"... impossible job," David was saying. "Don't think I don't know. But it has its rewards. I pay top money. I make provision for them in future. I provide first-rate accommodations. And in return"—his hand tightened on the wheelchair—"I expect loyalty. A sense that what goes on here is private."

He was trembling. Well, maybe she should tremble too. What made her suppose she could confide in him. David, whose few relationships have to make up for work, for sports, for sex, for the world. They're not just intense, these relationships, they're solemn. Not just solemn but sacrosanct. They carry a mandate for trust, faithfulness, concern, single-minded dedication. To impair them is tantamount, in his mind, to cutting him off.

She put a hand on his knee. "If this is how you feel, I'll go to the employment office today. See who we can get to replace him." She spoke fast, her sprightly tone negating the sinking heart. All of it starting again. The coded questions, the stolid answers, the wildly irrelevant references, the interminable session to explain about meals, medicines, therapy, living quarters, hours. And after all that, the setting up of appointments with David, and the overt impatience from the agency head whose advice is being ignored, and the tempered refusal to the applicant who strikes them as unsuitable, and the abrupt rejection from the one they both prefer—after someone is finally on the job, a frantic phone call from David. Maggie, we made a terrible mistake. It won't work out. Get someone else.

"Yes, do that, I'd really appreciate—No, Maggie, don't."

"Don't?" For a second—a wild ecstatic second—she thought his concern was for her.

"Let him stay." The square chin was set, the blue eyes looked bleakly ahead. "I want to find out."

"David, what—"

"I'll work on it. I'll be like my sister. A whiz at asking questions. Isn't that your thing—prying answers out of people?"

"The people I interview want to talk." She spoke with feeble dignity. "They're dying to, it makes them feel important."

"Well, my subject won't know he's talking. Maggie, leave it to me. Lawrence and I, we have plenty of time."

He's correct there. It's what disability means: all those hours tied to someone you mistrust. A forced marriage. Worse than marriage. "What if he suspects you're pumping him," she said. "The two of you here alone, he can..." She doesn't want to think of the subtle cruelties a person taking care of David is in position to inflict.

"Don't you think I'm smart enough, Maggie? Me, your sly old brother?" His big good-looking face gave her his mocking grin.

She walked around the room, straightening a newspaper, moving an ashtray, running an exploratory finger across the windowsill. "Suppose you do find out, you think he did it. Then what?"

"I'll figure some way to fix him."

For a second she stared at him. Another gun? Oh, this is wild, now she's the one showing irrational distrust. But the vindictive look is there, the same as when he talked about Sandy. Maybe someone in his position has to have an object of hate. Someone on whom he can project the bitterness. It's what keeps him going. Pumps the adrenaline. "David, it's dumb, it's demeaning, I wish you would forget it. I mean, if you really have these feelings about Lawrence, let's fire him, I'll get someone else, we surely—"

But she heard the elevator: another second and the door opened. Lawrence. Lawrence with his trained punctilio, his brazen tact, his elaborate explanations. The tailor said Friday, maybe Thursday, for the blue pants, but some complication with the tan ones seeing as how Mr. Bynam wants cuffs, so if Mr. Bynam would like to call himself, here's the number, the two of them can go into it. Meanwhile, since he was passing, he stopped at that pastry shop Mr. Bynam likes, their special coffee cake here in the box, so if Mrs. Berringer will wait a second while he gets plates . . .

"Oh, Lawrence, thanks. Sounds nice, but I have to run."
True enough. She has to run because all at once she feels she will suffocate in this room, this tabernacle to infirmity, this shrine for inflamed sensibilities, where the whiz at asking questions has been able to come up with none of the answers.

EIGHT

SHE WAITED TILL two days after the funeral to go to see Myra. Discreet condolence call. Not so close to the tragic event as to appear pushy, but also not so distant that a visit would seem uncaring. But she felt a pang as she rang the bell, because this was not a standard condolence call, or at least it was not only that, and following the maid, she walked stiffly, as though her ulterior motives were a blemish Myra could instantly perceive.

But Myra greeted her with quiet pleasure. Margaret was so good to come. There had been people here earlier, and some folks were stopping by at five, but middle of the afternoon was an empty time. Yesterday too. Maybe people thought you'd be wanting to rest then, but people were wrong; she felt better with company around.

"Sit here, it's more comfortable." Myra gave an absent smile. She was wearing a long, dark floppy dress at variance with the perfectly ordered room, and her hair was also floppy, falling in loose waves from a part in the middle. But she had an ordained role, grieving widow, and she said all the things a widow does. Paean to her late husband. Sandy had been remarkable. What a tragedy for him to be cut off. And really just making a mark in his career: all that talent for manipulating space. Well, take this room, even though it's just a minor example. Cozy with just the two of them, isn't it? Well, how many does Margaret think it can seat? Fifteen? Try again. Twenty-five, that's a fact. But nothing awkward or conspicuous, that's how skillful he was.

"And not just designing. That genius for communicating—that was his great gift. All he had to do was wave his

hands, and people were sold." Myra pushed back her hair.
"He had a miracle personality."

"Oh, I know."

"You don't, really. Just meeting him that one night." She
paused. Tears now? But the pause was just for the maid, a
somber woman named Helene who came in with a tray for
tea. "You'll have some, won't you? Or would you rather
something else? Coffee? A drink? That woman," she said
when the maid had closed the door. "Typical."

"Typical?"

"Of Sandy. This big house, I had trouble finding someone to do the work. Maybe you know how it is. Anyhow, we
went to Bermuda last year for vacation. Why Bermuda?
Sandy's choice, even though you'd think he would prefer
someplace more, I don't know, dashing. So we were down
there, and Sandy came back to the hotel one afternoon and
said I have one. A maid. Don't ask me how he found her or
what he offered or why she would just pick up and come to
New York. I didn't believe she would. No friends or family
here, nothing. But sure enough, a week after we got home,
the bell rings and there she is. This big sort of sad-looking
woman ready for work, with her apron and low-heeled shoes
in a paper bag." Myra poured the tea. That Sandy, she went
on. He could sell anyone.

Margaret nodded. It was also David's feeling, she point-
edly said.

Myra put down the cup. "Yes," she said. "David."

There was nothing remotely accusing about her voice, just
the same note of wistful blandness, but Margaret sat
straighter. "Listen. David didn't kill him." Her set piece
from now on: resolute, unequivocal, didactic.

"Didn't he?" Myra turned her absent, accommodating
face.

"I know there's been stuff in the papers. David Bynam
questioned, and David Bynam injured a year ago, and David Bynam cherishing an unavoidable hostility. And it's

true, he did drive out there, he was there just that morning. But they realize he didn't do it, the police accept that." Do they? She picked up a cup and set it down.

"Your poor brother—all that questioning must be a misery for him."

"Yes." Actually, that was not true. There had been two sessions after the one at the police station. Lengthy inquisitions when detectives came to David's apartment and hurled question after question. The car, the route, the time, the gun, the bridge where he allegedly threw the gun—reporting to her on these, he was incensed, but not only that. So I told them... Then they asked... If they have to know... As he went through the litany of interrogation, it seemed to her that his speech took on new vigor, his eyes shone, even his skin tone seemed to her in some indefinable way changed. He was enjoying it, she thought. No, not quite right. He hated it but he was also exhilarated by it. For over a year, as a matter of principle, he had systematically, assiduously, cut himself off from the world, but now an accusation of murder had brought him, willy-nilly, back into it. His name was in the newspapers. His telephone rang. In the police officers, he had found visitors who could not be discouraged. As a suspect, he was part of things, even though they might be undesirable things.

Nor had he again mentioned the bout with Lawrence, in which he was in the position, though the furtive one, of interrogator. Had he given up on that suspicion? Reconciled himself to it? Was he still going after the facts? Something else she didn't know, didn't see her way clear to finding out.

"Your poor brother," Myra repeated. "I hope you can get someone else to look into that swimming pool for him."

Margaret blinked. That pool again—how she keeps forgetting it.

"I really tried to reach Sandy," Myra said. "I was on the phone half a dozen times. Once I just missed him. He'd been at this hotel and checked out that afternoon. It must have been what I said—something offended him. The color of the walls or the furniture in the lobby—I told you about those finicky standards. And he didn't leave a forwarding number or maybe he did, but you know those hotels, too disorganized to get anything straight.''

"Myra, it's all right.'' What's she saying! It's not all right. Myra's husband is dead. Suppose that hotel had found the number—would he now be alive?

"And Ken couldn't find him either? You did go to Ken?'' Myra asked in her languid voice. "Funny, Ken not knowing about his own partner. I mean, a business trip, a partner should by rights be in touch, shouldn't he? So you can't help wondering. Was there any—well, it's silly to speculate, isn't it? But you would think, if one half of a firm goes off to Chicago, the other half would know where to get hold of him. Here, let me give you some more tea.''

She spilled a little on the table as she poured, but she didn't seem conscious of the stain, anymore than she seemed conscious of the import of what she was saying. She only looked up when Margaret said she'd also gone to Simon.

"And Simon flubbed it too? Even though the two of them were so close, always keeping tabs on each other. I mean, hardly a day when they didn't talk on the phone, sometimes two or even three times.'' The droopy head slumped lower, above the baggy dress. "Except they didn't exchange visits, there was that. Simon and that stunning wife and those two adorable kids, I don't think they've set foot in this house for almost a year. And we never went there. Don't ask me why. We just never went. Maybe Simon being so rich, millions from that law practice, everyone says, all that money gets in the way. Or maybe it's just brothers. Love/hate. Except not really brothers,'' Myra went placidly on. "Simon was adopted. He's just a year older—I always figured it must be one of those classic cases. You know. The wife can't have a baby, and can't have one, and finally she decides to go the adoption route, and just after the new baby is installed, she finds she's pregnant." Myra smoothed down her dress, as though smoothing away the insinuations. That great medley of facts given, facts modified, facts suggested and retracted and held in tantalizing incompletion—in the same bland voice she had poured it all out.

Simon had been very nice these last few days, she added. Supportive. He had her come down to the office and went over papers and told her if there was any help she needed, financial, that is, to tide her over the next year . . .

"Myra, will you need help?"

"Not really. Sandy had insurance. Besides, you just never know what will turn up. Yesterday I went to the bank, and imagine. Just two days before he went away, Sandy deposited a hundred thousand dollars. Just like that. An honest to God hundred thousand that had nothing to do with the office."

"Are you sure?"

"Oh, positive. Sandy had already deposited his share for the month. Ken should know, after all. How much came in, how much was left after expenses. And Sandy had no other source of income, stocks or anything, or I would know about that."

"What did Ken say?"

"He clammed up. No help at all. But he wasn't pleased. I've known him a long time, so I could see the little signs. Something about the whole business that had that nice Kenneth Ash gritting his teeth."

"Did you tell the police?"

A look of unaccustomed slyness from under the veil of hair. "I guess you've never had someone be killed," Myra said. "You don't have to tell things to the police, it seems they know as soon as you do, before you do."

"What did they say?"

"They said I should look in other places, maybe there was more. So I did. I went down to our vault this morning. But nothing. Look, I'll show you, here's the whole lot." She made her languid way to the desk and back. "A medal from college he won for track, and his stamp album, and some old coins, but I don't think they're worth much—oh, and this watch that belonged to his grandfather. Sandy never would wear it but he said we might as well keep it safe. And that's it. No, here's a clipping from twenty-five years ago. A hospital dedicated when they were all in Bermuda for vacation. Sandy and Simon and his parents. His father was a big wheel in some pharmaceutical company. I suppose he gave the money for this hospital even though the paper's torn; his name isn't on it."

Margaret picked up the medal. Plain, bronze, with faded blue ribbon. Two-hundred-yard dash. "Nice," she murmured.

"I don't know why he had to have a vault. All this stuff could perfectly well have gone in some bottom drawer. That stamp album, for instance, nothing valuable. Even the watch, not antique or eighteen karat or anything. But he was sentimental, Sandy was. Yes, it's true, at heart a real softie."

Another statement she might as easily retract ten minutes later. But the sentimental spoils were indubitably here, and because Myra seemed to expect it, Margaret picked up each piece in turn. The album, the coins, the watch, the torn clipping in its plastic case. "Wing of North Montclair Hospital. Dedicated Today. Doctors hope that with the new facilities for surgery and the added research laboratory..." She turned it over, but no family name there either, just the standard items from any resort newspaper: "After forty years under Hanover family ownership, Stone Haven Restaurant changing hands." "Export figures for this year grow by 1.08%." "Chambermaid at the Seacliff Hotel who was sexually assaulted by eighteen-year-old guest is now in guarded condition.'' ''Weller Commission to report on beach erosion next week.''

She stood up. She had wanted insight into Sandy Fleming's life, his murder, but she wouldn't find it in these relics exhumed from their pretentious burial place. Well, then, how did you end a condolence call?

But Myra was ahead of her. On the way out, maybe Margaret would like to see the studio, such a great place, the slanting walls and sensational window . . . She spoke in the prescriptive tone that can be a tactic of the habitually languid: Do it my way, *please*.

Well, of course she'll do it, especially since she abjured the studio on her first visit. She'll do it although she knows that studio means not just the walls and window but the works produced therein: a guided tour of the paintings.

They stood in bins on the floor, these paintings; they hung on every inch of wall space; they were stacked against the two easels, a few fitting into a cleverly designed shelf above the door. Ten years' work, Myra said. Since she and Sandy were married. But not all the same kind of work; Margaret could see the changes. This stack here—goodness, so dusty—mostly floral studies. The rounded shapes juxtaposed against the severity of geometric backgrounds, that was her gimmick at the time. And here—just a second till she moved this box—these were marine landscapes. Fishing villages. She and Sandy were on a trip to Maine. She did sketches on the spot and then worked up the paintings when they got home. And over here, well, her abstract period, Margaret might not be so interested, and anyhow, she's dropped this style completely. And here, against the easel, back to landscapes, but Margaret can see the difference, this time she worked at capturing the quality of light at different hours.

Myra positioned herself beside an easel. Come up with an opinion, her gaze said. What do you think?

What Margaret thought was that the paintings were like the painter. Soft-focus, blurry, indeterminate; they didn't aim for sharpness or precision. The green triangle on a purple background seemed as arbitrary, as detached from some governing logic, as her opinions: She knew where Sandy was, she didn't know; Sandy and Simon got on well, they didn't get on; Kenneth Ash cherished some private anger against Sandy, he and Sandy were trusted partners.

Myra was waiting. "Really an interesting collection," Margaret said.

"These last, I think I got a whole new feeling of solidity in the rocks."

Oh, Margaret agreed, she certainly did.

Colors and shapes pressed in on her, a luxuriant jungle. "Pick one," Myra suddenly said. "Go on, I'd like you to have it."

"Myra, I can't possibly..."

"One of these later ones? Or maybe you'd like a floral, go better with your room at home. Just say which, I'll have Helene come in and wrap it."

Margaret edged toward the door. Assigning a preference implies granting a commendation. I like that one best—it means, it can't help meaning, I liked others too, I had a devil of a time deciding, I couldn't choose between this and that blue one over by the wall. Besides, an involvement is augmented; whether the painting is hung on a wall or consigned behind old raincoats in a closet, a bit of the painter is implacably with you, the one who did the fishing villages has moved into your life.

"Myra, I'd love one, I really would. But not this moment...going someplace...no way to carry...I mean, if I could have a rain check."

But she knew from the look of dismay on the soft face that she had erred, she had hurt Myra in perhaps the only place where she was vulnerable.

NINE

"NO, DARLING," she said to Erica. "I can't make lunch to-morrow, Ken Ash said I should come around one."

"Ken Ash, he's Sandy's partner, isn't he? And yesterday you went to see Sandy's wife."

This was the time to add that today—in roughly an hour, in fact—she was going to see Sandy's brother. "Yes, con-dolence call," she said. "You never met Myra, did you? Nice enough woman, but droopy, listless, maybe it's from lack of confidence, or maybe just the opposite, an innate feeling of being somehow above it all, but anyhow, nothing is censored, it all comes out, nothing matters more than anything else unless you want to count her awful paint-ings."

She might have known that coy effusiveness wouldn't help. "Mom, which are you doing? Paying condolence calls or playing detective?"

Judicious silence. They had just had the arranged brunch with David, which predictably was an hour devoted to Da-vid's problems, which had led to Erica's saying why couldn't the two of them have time alone tomorrow, which was why Erica was now stopped on the street to regard her mother with a look of quizzical inquiry.

The street was empty, or half empty. New York on a spring Sunday morning: a scene devoid of the usual rush, anxiety, derangement. Those few who are around walk slowly, sporting print dresses, straw hats, flowers in buttonholes, navy in all its haughty permutations. Erica, who was due at her clinic in five minutes, had on a navy skirt, navy sweater, red eyelet blouse. Plus, of course, the challenging expression, which Margaret now tried to placate. "Just because I—"

"Because you go to people you hardly know on errands you can barely justify. Mom, want to come in? That group won't start for ten minutes."

Yes, she wanted to come in. Especially if once inside the conversation would veer from the disquieting course on which Erica had it headed. But though she paused for her usual admiring look at the congenial warren of small rooms that constituted the Rape Intervention Center, when they sat in Erica's office, nothing had changed. "Honestly, Mom." Erica's voice of dogged certitude. "Detective work. You think it's like work you get paid to do. Sampling the opinions of eighty-five people in a ten-block area. Do you belong to a country club? Do you have the newspaper delivered? Which section do you read first? But the questions you ask after a murder" —she shook off her sweater to reveal the short-sleeved eyelet blouse— "do you really think, just because a nice-looking and sympathetic woman asks them, people are going to come clean? A full disclosure? They're going to tell you what they went to great lengths not to let on to the police? Oh, my sweet mother, you really are deluding yourself."

She sat stiffly on the cane-backed chair. Part of her feels tight with anger: at this point the last thing she needs is discouragement. But part of her, on the other hand, melts with delight. Erica is protecting her, just as she protects others who come into this room. Margaret has moved under that capacious umbrella; she's eligible for the interest and solicitude this room has been set up to provide.

"Anyhow, Mom, why would you want to do it? They're not going to indict David, not a chance." Erica pushed back her hair. This is the way she sits all day, her loveliness subdued into an informed sternness. "Oh, they'll keep questioning him, why not, he's the obvious suspect. But they don't want him on their hands. God, no. Why saddle themselves with someone like him when all they have to say is it was some unknown burglar, someone who got caught by Sandy in the act, and the investigation has so far turned up some promising leads.''

''They're tormenting him with all that questioning.''

Erica shook her head. ''You know what I think? He kind of likes it. Oh, he'd never say it, he'd deny it, he probably doesn't know it himself. But look at the way he was today. His voice, for once, with a little life in it. It's a change, that's what, the first he's had in over a year, something to stir up that deadly routine.''

So she noted it too. What a girl. It's not just women she understands, those who sit here frightened or frigid or clammed up; she saw through David when he leaned forward in his wheelchair and said, ''Those bastards, why don't they leave me alone?''

''So, Mom, quit, will you? Before you get yourself in trouble?''

''Well...''

''In trouble with your job too, I bet. All this time away from the office, aren't they pissed off?''

''I'm taking two weeks.'' There was a pamphlet on the desk—''Crisis and Recovery''—and she fingered it. ''I want to be free to spend time with David if he needs me.''

That quizzical look again. ''Also, to have lunch with Ken Ash. What's he like anyhow?''

''Very nice, actually. A talented clever nice architect.'' She stopped. Any more will get into a discussion of how she knows about all that niceness, which will lead to a revelation of that first visit, which is something she is determined that Erica, with all her intuition, not find out about.

''I really know,'' Erica said.

''Know what?''

''Why you're doing this. The meetings, the visits, the lunches. My Mom, super detective. It's not for David at all, it's for you. You know he didn't do it, you absolutely believe him, but you can't help thinking he might have. Especially because of that gun. A gun that a man throws where it can't be found, such a dumb thing to do, for heaven's sake, or is it a very smart thing, was there something about that gun he didn't want anyone to know, like what kind of bullets and were any of them fired? Anyhow, there they are, the tantalizing questions, so if you can just find out for sure."

She flipped through the pamphlet. Definition of mother-daughter relationship, she thought. Each sees through the other, knows her better than she may find it convenient to be known. She murmured something deprecating, but the picture slid into her head, the picture she will never entirely expunge: David with bent elbow and steely eye at the car window, while against the background of sand and grass a man stands panicked, mesmerized.

"Do you have a candidate?"

"Erica, don't be foolish."

"You must think someone. The brother? The partner? The wife? What's your guess?"

"Erica, I'm not—"

"Actually, his wife—what's her name? Maura? Myra? From one point of view, she's the one with reason to kill him— Oh, Lori, tell them to start without me, I'll be there in two minutes."

What they were starting was a group that involved role playing. After rape they're turned off sex, so this is a tactic to get them to the state where it can give them gratification again—this was the way Erica had explained it as they walked along that festive street, and all at once she'd remembered Myra: Your own daughter, don't you mind? Okay, at that moment she did mind. She looked at the pretty girl beside her and thought, maybe she's also an appropriate candidate for that therapy. She sits all day listening to the stories, appropriating them, empathizing with the victims. It's not like being a victim herself, but the process must take its toll. And it was a fact, now she looked back, that Erica had gone with unaccustomed rapidity through a succession of partners this past year. There was the theatrical agent and the poet who made a living teaching high school Latin and the man who ran his father's furniture business into the ground and the orthopedic surgeon who wanted to make Erica his third wife and more, more—could it be that this great inconstancy implied something more deep-seated than simple caprice? Erica, honey, does it get to you after a while, hearing all those squalid details, so you find yourself unable to...unable... Impossible. Not a question a mother can phrase to a daughter. Anyhow, not this mother.

Actually, it was just this reluctance to speak about certain subjects to Erica that had been at the heart of one of the worst fights between her and Alex. It went on for a shorter period than the suburb/city *kampf*, it involved fewer physical rearrangements than the disclosure about his love affair, it found her less imbued with pious fervor than the battle about her going to work. But in some ways it aroused the most bitterness because it was about what they both cared for most, which was their daughter.

And it started with deceptive calm. That is, there was no great impact when Erica announced one day that now she had her degree she was planning to set up something called a rape intervention clinic. Alex even asked patient and intelligent questions. What good could a rape intervention clinic perform and why was another one needed and who would fund it and where would it be located, and since Erica had been saying she wanted to be financially independent, could she expect it to pay her a living wage? It wasn't till they were alone that he let loose. Why hadn't Margaret said anything?

"About what?"

"It's a crazy idea. Bizarre."

"Actually, it's a very high-minded, public-spirited idea."

"Then let someone else have it. Not my daughter. She doesn't know what she's letting herself in for."

"Oh, Alex, I doubt that. That responsible girl, if she takes up a project." Stalling, speaking with insolent slowness because she sensed what was smoldering up ahead, she went through the familiar litany of Erica's responsibleness: chosen head of this at college and graduate school, president of that, voted best at something else, given such and such awards.

"Job like that, someone should be older. Less impressionable."

"Someone older might not want to go through the headaches involved in getting an agency started."

"She'll feel degraded. She'll hate it."

"No, she won't. Well, sometimes maybe she will. It's one of the problems she'll have to handle."

Something about her ambivalence, her resigned lassitude, sent him into a passion. His voice got blustering, then vicious. "You sit there so damn sanguine. As if you like it. Well, admit, you do like it. You're getting what you really want. That's it, isn't it, she's playing out some dream of yours. You couldn't give public service yourself so you have her doing it. Your daughter as surrogate."

At sight of the weary disgust in her face he got more worked up. "And where will it lead? As if I didn't know. She'll marry some deadbeat. Another of your fantasies. What you really wanted for yourself, isn't it? Not a successful businessman, oh, no. Someone unrealistic, head in the clouds, no drive, no ambition."

She sat there stricken, thinking he didn't mean what he was saying. No. He meant something worse. It had nothing to do with Erica. It was a tirade against her, Margaret, against all the times when she had been faulty, lacking; she hadn't given him his rightful share of sex or sympathy; she was not the sweet, loving wife he felt justified in expecting. I didn't really want you, is what he was saying. I wanted someone softer, more compliant, someone, I don't know, different.

She looked at him with coldness. "You're not the least concerned about Erica's welfare. It's all you. Your selfish, self-centered vanity. Why don't you say what you really have against this job?"

"I don't want my daughter having anything to do with a rape clinic. Simple as that. I don't have to go into details."

"If you feel so strongly, why didn't you tell her? Why'd you sit there all approving and interested, collecting brownie points for being such a tolerant father?"

"It's your place to tell her."

Ah: the crux of it. "I should be the bitchy one, the one she gets to resent."

"If you really loved her you'd be willing to speak out."

She didn't even bother to answer that. Besides, he suddenly changed his tactic. He could do that. In the middle of the most unreasoning vehemence, stand next to her, lower his voice, assume a look of gentle ruefulness, even let an arm lower itself around her shoulder, as if it had slid there of its own accord. "Tell the truth, Maggie. Wouldn't you rather have her at some other job?"

Yes. The truth was yes. True then and still, at certain times, true now. She looked sideways at her daughter in her perky red and blue outfit and thought, why can't she have a job designing store windows, or catering parties, or doing layout for a fashion magazine?

"What's that about Myra's reason?" she said.

"Just that Sandy was playing around. You didn't know? A friend of mine. Louise—do you remember? It was her cousin. Sandy and the girl had this thing for a year."

"Erica, you never told me."

"What was to tell? He did what we needed, plans for this classy office, what was the big deal?"

She looked around: the clever solution for what had been a difficult space. No big deal.

"And after her cousin, Louise said, some young lawyer. Or did she say med student? Anyhow, after her, someone out of town."

"Chicago!" It came out too fast, with too much of a rush of feeling. The gray eyes looked her over.

"Mom, will you drop it? You promise? Oh, Lord, I have to run."

She ran just on time; another second and she'd have elicited that promise. But the group was starting, the session intended to give women back their ability to get gratification from the sexual encounter, and it was desirable for the director of the clinic to attend, and this left Margaret free to go ahead with what she had planned, which was to pick up her rented car and drive to Westchester to see Simon Fleming.

She drove slowly, following without trouble the instructions the man at the car rental place wrote out, half hoping she would lose her way or the car would break down or some other mishap beyond her control would make the decision for her. But nothing intervened, and by half past two she was at the plainly marked gate on the wide, curving, tree-lined street viewing the scene on the lawn beyond. Sunday afternoon in suburbia: for a second tears came to her eyes. She had never wanted to live anyplace but the city, city kids turn out best, was what she had told herself all the years when Erica was growing up, but with a pang she thought, this is what we missed. Every detail carved out of some emblematic representation entitled Perfect Family: the father batting the ball so it dribbles tamely across the grass, the two small boys squealing with pleasure as they dash to make the catch, the mother with her calm smile and sun-flushed face above the plate of juice and doughnuts.

And no strain. Not even any strain when a newcomer drives up. Why, it's Mrs. Berringer, Simon said, and the scene modulated into another: from active play to courteous greeting in three easy seconds. A greeting that didn't go on for too long. The father put down the bat, the boys as if on schedule disappeared through a gap in the shrubbery, the mother, after a few nice words, said she had to see about something in the house. Tact, tact. Well, he wouldn't have gotten where he was unless his family knew the time and mechanics for making themselves scarce.

He was tactful too. He was so glad she'd come; he'd been wanting to talk to her. Yes, he knew how she felt about Sandy. It was terrible, terrible. Now, would she like to go in the house, or, this splendid day, would she rather sit out here where— Well, then, this bench. Be quiet.

It was not exactly quiet. There were shouts from the adjoining lawn, where the game had obviously reconstituted itself, and hortatory chirping from some birds, and the ping of tennis balls from a nearby court, but it seemed quiet. Margaret leaned back on the rustic wood. Simon makes millions, Myra had said—maybe this is what it means: not the spacious lawn, the lavish shrubbery, the large mock-Tudor house, but the assurance that every vignette will automatically compose itself into something pleasing, picturesque.

She pointed to a flower bed, where red and white flowers thrived in calculated confusion. "Beautiful. I wish I knew their names.

"When I lived in the city, the only names of flowers I knew where the tags at the corner florist. Three for two-ninety-five. One-fifty apiece." He picked up a child's sweater and folded it. "The truth is, I still don't know them. The flowers are Dianne's department, she does the beds."

Of course. She'd do everything right, that woman with the serene good looks. "I used to know trees at least—there was a girl scout merit badge—but I've forgotten even that."

He said the great swooping branches they were sitting under belonged to a copper beech. Then he turned. "You didn't come to talk about trees, did you, Mrs. Berringer?"

Well. The business of the afternoon underway at last. "I did want to tell you how terrible I feel about your brother. I thought it was the least I could do, after all your helpfulness last time. And also" —she spoke quickly, it had to be done fast— "I wanted to talk about my brother. Thing is," she imperatively said, "David didn't do it."

"Oh, I believe you." Not the obliging and halfhearted assent of Myra, one stringing along in the interests of hospitality, but a vigorous affirmation, the sunburned face under the boyish haircut giving an emphatic nod.

"I know he felt very strongly that Sandy had injured him. By now, thanks to the newspapers, everyone knows. But he didn't kill him. He's not that kind. Commit murder! Shoot someone! David couldn't do it, nothing in his makeup would allow it."

"Well, I'm sure—"

"Besides, he admired Sandy. He really did. Oh, he was furious at him, of course. He thought Sandy's negligence had ruined him. But he knew exactly what kind of person Sandy was. You don't kill someone you think is likable and talented and charming."

"Mrs. Berringer, I'm on your side. You don't have to convince me." Simon Fleming leaned back. A dynamo, Erica had said. Well, even while he's dressed in sneakers, tan slacks, a flannel shirt with sleeves rolled up, the dynamic presence is apparent. "You want to know what I really think? Some passing burglar shot Sandy. Someone who saw the inviting target of an empty house and figured there might be something worth hauling off and was surprised to find that that half-finished structure was temporarily not empty after all. And after a few more days, having posed all the ritual questions and explored all the mandatory dead ends, the police will come to the same conclusion and that will be that."

She pulled at a piece of grass. A burglar certified first by Erica and now, in his magisterial way, by Simon—for an instant the man was real. He drove a red pickup truck. He wanted to add a room to the dilapidated house where he lived with his wife and child. He had three felonies on his record, so a fourth would finish him. When Sandy surprised him he shot in a frenzy of anger and apprehension.

"You really think that's what will happen?"

Yes, he really did.

"Suppose the police find out Sandy came home from Chicago four days ahead of schedule?"

Simon's voice was even. A man on a business trip was entitled to an unannounced change of plans; that shouldn't get him killed.

"Suppose they also find out that three people close to him couldn't locate him at the places they had every right to expect he would be?"

A sidelong glance, half rueful, half admiring, was turned on her. "You're an interesting woman, Mrs. Berringer. Your instinct wants you to accept the theory of an armed intruder at the same time as your intellect forces you to inquire what chance that theory has of holding up."

"I'm just trying to look at it from all the angles the police will."

"Way to do it," he murmured.

"Well, Myra did tell me she tried the most likely hotel. I assume she'd also tell the police." She sucked on the stem of grass—how odd to find it tasting the same as grass did twenty years ago. "And you didn't get hold of him either, isn't that right?"

Simon shook his head. It was true that Sandy hadn't made the call, the important call, he promised to make, and that he himself hadn't had time to get the hotel chain working on his plan.

When she paused, the noises from beyond the hedge seemed louder. "Safe! I was *so* safe!" a boy's voice shrieked.

"I understand—well, do you think it's possible that instead of going to some conference, Sandy was seeing a woman in Chicago?"

Simon bent down, the big impressive head resting on his open palms. "Oh, it's sad, isn't it? Die an untimely death— I guess it's inevitable—and your private life becomes public." He turned on her another of the rueful looks. "About a Chicago woman specifically I can't say, but yes, Sandy had other women. He never told me anything specific, but he knew I guessed it. He was a very attractive guy. And Myra— well, she's a nice person, I always liked her, but you wouldn't exactly call her a charmer."

He liked her, but for a year he had not visited her—the thought briefly impinged. "Did Myra know?"

"I'm not sure. My hunch is she didn't know in the beginning. But lately—well, if you made the deduction, Mrs. Berringer, it's hard to see how a wife, working on considerably more evidence, could have avoided the suspicion."

"Did she mind?"

Did Myra mind? Reflectively, a man who valued accuracy, Simon took time to roll down the sleeves of his flannel shirt. "Mrs. Berringer, you saw Myra. Does she strike you as the kind of woman who would cope with having a husband leave her? Would she care, for example, to launch out for herself, carve out a new life, even conceivably find a new man?"

The thought crossed her mind that she should tell him to call her Margaret. Two civilized people sitting on a rustic bench discussing topics of some intimacy—good manners practically demand it. But actually she doesn't want to be Margaret; a whiz at asking questions—someone who must be sure of remaining a whiz at asking questions—had best remain within the confines of Mrs. Berringer.

"A woman without even a career to sustain her," Simon went on. "Unless you count those paintings—Oh, excuse me." Because Dianne was calling. Harry Someone was on the phone, did Simon want—

Simon wanted. His big figure moved easily across the grass. She stood and looked around. Acres and acres, all culminating in that half-timbered facade with the tall, shaped chimneys and projecting bays. If they had moved to the country when Alex wanted to, Erica would have grown up in one of these houses where perennial games go on across hospitable lawns. She'd have ridden in a chaperoned car pool to dancing school and made best friends with girls whose mothers Margaret knew and gone off for one rationed day a month to the city. She wouldn't now—it was conceivable, wasn't it?—be running a clinic for rape victims.

"Dianne says she wishes you'd come in." Simon was back.

She considered it briefly. The decorated rooms, the agreeable hostess, tea served on a porch fragrant with sun and flowers. She said no thanks, in a minute she had to leave.

"What were we talking about?"

"Myra. Myra left alone without Sandy." She closed her eyes for a second; this wasn't going to be easy. "I asked her if she'd be able to make out financially, and she told me Sandy had made a surprise deposit of a hundred thousand dollars before he left for Chicago."

When Simon moved, sun filtered through the overhead branches to fall in abstract slashes across his face. "You're no amateur when it comes to getting information, are you, Mrs. Berringer?"

She said honestly that her questions hadn't been expert as much as Myra's talk had been voluminous.

"Well, the fact is, she told me too. A windfall."

"Any idea where Sandy would get that kind of money? I mean, over and beyond what he drew from the firm?"

Simon shrugged. "I have lots of ideas, but do I know? That is, if a lawyer managed to get hold of a sizable bundle that wasn't part of his legitimate income, I could come up with some knowledgeable speculation. But an architect? I can only guess. Same as you."

"Are you implying that Sandy might have been getting money from some illegal transaction?"

"Don't pin me to the wall, Mrs. Berringer. It's my brother we're talking about."

Brother by adoption—it went through her mind. "Did Sandy say anything to you about the money?"

"Not directly. Now I realize he was in effect telling me. He said on the phone the day he left that he was planning to make some big changes in his life. I asked did that mean he was leaving Myra, and he didn't confirm anything but he didn't issue denials either. Then I said where would he get the money, meaning of course money to settle on Myra while he supported a second establishment, and he said money had stopped being a problem. I don't know why I'm telling you all this, Mrs. Berringer. Just because you sit there with that wide-eyed look on your attractive face."

"Please keep telling me."

"There's nothing more to tell. Unless you want to go into my expressions of disapprobation. I did say I hoped he would watch his step, or at least do so for the next couple of months."

"That nomination..."

"You guessed it," Simon Fleming said with his endearing candor. "I don't want trouble. Not now, when the smallest thing can tip the balance. And the fact is, if Caesar's wife has to be above reproach, so does Caesar's brother."

His voice gave way to another—"Hey, Daddy, you ever coming?" Simultaneously, a small figure burst through the shrubbery to deliver a tearful story. Someone had slid, and that stone they put up for second base, and Mr. Hamill's different rules—saga of aggrieved defeat.

She was suddenly abashed. He's probably allotted this one hour to his children, squeezed in between the meetings and phone calls and conferences and speeches. "Listen. I'll be going now."

"Don't worry. They can wait. I wouldn't have taken the time if I didn't feel a certain admiration for your mission." He walked with her across the lawn. "I just hope you got what you were after," he said as he opened her car door. "I also hope your brother appreciates what you're doing for him."

"I hope he never finds out."

"If he does, tell him one observer thinks you're very gutsy. A real gutsy lady. I can't promise to agree with your conclusions, but as they say in the books, I respect your right, et cetera, et cetera. So go to it, Mrs. Berringer," he said cheerfully. "More power to you."

TEN

NEXT DAY KENNETH ASH was also cheerful. "Did the wind slay you?" He met her at the door of his office.

"Fierce, isn't it?"

"Penalty we pay for a river view—here, let me have your coat."

"Is it like this every day?"

"Just about. That's why I said don't walk to Riverside, meet me at the restaurant."

"I wasn't sure what time I could come," she said quickly.

"Whenever you come is the right time. Sit here while I put this stuff away."

But she stood, she walked around, looking at the drawings. Old friends, on this second visit. The intensive care unit, the Midwest college complex, the resort house, the police precinct with its intimation of the shiny blue police cars. "This is a new one," she said. "At least I don't remember it."

"You're a good observer. It is new." He was standing next to her. "Bar and restaurant. These zigzag lines on the diagonal, that's the bar, we thought we'd put it out on the center of the floor. Very daring."

"And up here is the restaurant?"

"Right. Up this sort of grandiose staircase. Sandy wanted a splash, drama on the way to dinner; he was working on it before he went away."

She took a deep breath. "Is that one of the drawings he took out to Chicago? On that nonbusiness business trip?"

"What are you talking about?" Ken moved back to his desk.

"Sandy's last trip. His trip to Chicago to see a woman."

"Where'd you get that idea?" That edgy tone—how fast it had superseded the warmly welcoming one of a minute before.

"From Myra. From you too if it comes to that. Because neither of you could get hold of him, and I suspect you knew when you talked to me that you wouldn't be able to get hold of him. All that about his famous unpredictability—Myra knew he wouldn't be at any hotel, and you knew he had no intention of sitting in on discussions about homes for the homeless."

Ken shrugged. "If it's true, why should it matter? It's not so unusual. A married man who has a woman in another town."

"It's not usual for a man to come home from that town and be shot."

Ken rolled up a drawing and fitted it into a cardboard container. "How the hell did we get into this?"

"I'm sorry. I didn't mean..."

"It's okay. We're all overwrought. It's true. Knowing Sandy, I think there may well have been a woman, and if the police want to rake it over, that's their business. So now can we get out of here before the restaurant's too crowded?"

She said sure, but she didn't move. She said this hypothetical woman was not the only topic appropriate for the official raking over.

He had picked up his jacket but he put it down. "Now what?"

"Myra told me Sandy deposited a mysterious hundred thousand dollars before he left."

"How'd that get to be a subject between you and Myra?"

"I paid a condolence call."

Ken slipped the container next to a pile of others on an open shelf. "A standard condolence call, and she told you about Sandy's bank deposits?"

"No secret." She heard the defiant note in her own voice: something about the whole business to make that nice Ken Ash grit his teeth. "The police know all about it. They'd looked into his other accounts, they talked about it to you, they were satisfied it didn't represent any proper income from this office."

"What do you mean, proper?"

She looked out at the street. The tree at the curb was in leaf, sun splashed on its jaunty heart-shaped leaves. But three large branches were bare, she saw. Assaulted by drought, dogs, people, trash, this city child might or might not have the fortitude to make it through the coming summer.

When she turned, she said "proper" was Simon's word. Or had he said legal?

Ken smoothed the tissue paper tacked over the drawing on his desk. "Margaret, what are you up to?"

"I don't..."

"In the five minutes you've been here, you've asked two questions. What about some illicit affair Sandy maybe was carrying on and what about some illicit money he maybe was squirreling away? No, you didn't exactly ask them, you just sort of slid them into the conversation. Are you trying to play detective?"

She stood next to the daring zigzag bar. "Suppose I am. What's so wrong?"

"One thing is that all this coy indirection isn't like you, it spoils the kind of person you are. Another thing"—he looked not at her but at a yellow-painted duct along the ceiling—"well, it's not a job for you. It's for the police."

"Suppose the police don't feel any special urge to investigate?"

"How do you figure that?"

"They have David. From their point of view, the perfect suspect. Someone with motive and also means—obviously, he was in the right place at the right time. But also, they don't have to push it. I mean, no one in the world will be offended if someone like David isn't brought to justice. They have their man and they don't have him; they can leave it dangling. Best of all possible worlds.''

"Except not best, she thinks, for Margaret Berringer.''

She waited until his gaze met hers. "Why are you so against it?''

"Because you're trying to do something the police can do better. They have the training. They can force people to speak. They have techniques for assessing truth. Also, going around asking questions, they don't put themselves at risk.''

"I don't exactly feel at risk standing here.'' But he didn't return her smile.

"Margaret, listen. Once in a while someone comes up to me. So you're an architect, they say. Well, that's nice, but my brother built a house without one. He saw this plan and worked with the contractor himself, and you should see that house. Great place... Well, I don't believe it's all that great, but even if it is, I don't like it. I don't care to see architects bypassed. They work hard for their expertise and I want to see it utilized. I guess that's how I feel about the police. This case is their baby. Not yours. Theirs.''

She stood looking at him: the thin nose that twitched with displeasure, the eyebrows drawing closer. If she stopped it right now, they could still go on to that lunch. A duplicate of the last one, better than the last one. Imagination gave her the cluttered table, the people bent toward each other at the tables on either side, the look of tolerant amusement in Ken's gaze as she finished off first her salad and then his. After lunch he would say, I don't have to be back right away, so if you're also free....

"Simon knows what I'm doing,'' she said. "Sandy's brother. I was up there yesterday. He doesn't seem to mind.''

"Ah, the great Simon Fleming. The people's candidate. How do you think he got where he is? By being an automatic glad-hander, that's how. Say yes to everyone. Say yes even though you know damn well an hour later circumstances may be such that you'll have to say no."

But his tone suddenly changed. "That doesn't sound so nice, does it? Actually, it's not Simon I balk at, it's his type. Even that's not true. I simply realize I could never fit that type myself. Radiating easy cordiality, dispensing instant support—how do they stand it? But I understand that types like that are important; who'd sit in Washington getting our gripe mail if guys like Simon weren't willing to go through the mill?"

He heaved a sigh. "So now I got that off my chest, is there anything else you want to know? Because I've been looking forward to this lunch, and I don't relish the idea of an inquisitorial session between the soup and the meat balls."

She clenched her fist. Nothing should have to be this hard. "Yes. I want the name of the woman Sandy went to see in Chicago."

Back to that drawn, faintly grimacing face again, but he answered quietly. "I can be honest about that. I really don't know. Partners, but our talk didn't go along those lines. I assumed there was a woman, of course, all the secrecy hoopla, but I don't have a concrete fact."

She looked past him, to the drawing tacked on the wall behind his head. A terrace? A walled garden? Something, at any rate, he hadn't deemed worthy of exegesis last time. She spoke slowly. "If you're going to visit someone out of town, making arrangements, you want to phone them. Well, he wouldn't call from home. And no one in his right mind goes into a phone booth if he can help it. So if I could look over your phone bills for, say, the last couple of months, see if there's a Chicago number."

He spoke with no expression. The office had several Chicago contacts. How would she know which was the appropriate one?

"I'd need your help, of course. You'd have to go through your files, check off the numbers you recognized."

He sat down at his desk: man at work. "Is that why you wanted to meet me here instead of the restaurant? So you could take a look at last month's phone bill?"

She said that was part of it.

"Suppose you get her number, this hypothetical girl? Then what? Are you going to take her out to dinner? Console her for Sandy's loss? Or maybe she might have a line on where Sandy got that mysterious money."

So now he's throwing back at her her own petty theatrics. "I haven't decided yet."

"What will you say to her that the police can't say better?"

"The police aren't looking for her," she burst out. "They won't find her."

"But you know otherwise, you think it's important she be found."

"I think there's no way of knowing till we try."

"How about the potential damage if the trial goes bad?"

All right, she gives up. He won't help her unless she gives him a good reason, and she has no good reason; a good reason doesn't exist. She has only the matchstick words like hunch and instinct which would cut no ice with him, which in fact she had best not dwell on herself because they activate her own doubts. Oh, who would have expected him to turn out like this? There he sits, an expression of placid thoughtfulness on his face as if he were reflecting on the degree of grandiosity suitable for a restaurant stairway, but there's a solid core of stubbornness inside, no way around it.

When he looked up, the expression had not changed. "Okay, here's a bargain. You tell me why you were so fired up to get hold of Sandy; I'll do my best to put you on to this girl."

"But I told you. This company in Chicago working on an experimental swimming pool, so I thought if Sandy—"

"Margaret, come on."

"You don't believe it?"

"It's an explanation that has some holes. Such as why for something so important, you wouldn't go yourself."

"But I have no technical knowledge of that kind of thing, I couldn't possibly assess—"

"Or why with all your brother's connections you couldn't get a real expert on the subject of therapeutic pools to do an evaluation."

"But Sandy always said he was so anxious to be—"

"Or why it had to be just this trip. If Sandy was your man, why he couldn't turn around and go back to Chicago next week."

She drummed on the windowpane. "Why didn't you say all this the first time?"

"The first time an appealing woman came to my office with a story about wanting to see Sandy, and I very soon found I wanted to see her. That being so, why should I inquire closely into whether or not her story was wholly lucid?"

She said nothing.

"But once a man had been killed, shot, every detail, naturally, got to be significant. We looked at things differently. Scrutinized them. Searched them for plausibility."

"We?"

"Myra and Simon and I," he said.

"The three of you discussed this? You talked about me?"

"Be very strange if we hadn't. There we were, the three people you came to, the three most involved with Sandy's death."

The three witches, she thought suddenly. Each was capable of treating her in a courteous, almost a gracious manner. But interspersed in their hospitable broth were little chunks of malice, slipped in so casually, so adroitly, you hardly noticed them as they went down. Simon let fall that his brother might have been capable of illegal practices. Myra hinted that Simon was not a wholly loving brother and that Ken would have harbored ill will because of that bank deposit. Ken characterized Simon in distinctly unflattering terms.

"I talked to Myra and Simon both. Neither of them mentioned anything about not having believed me."

The telltale eyebrows twisted up. "Simon is professionally nice—we discussed that. It's not nice to tell a woman you think her carefully wrought story may just be rubbish. As for Myra, she's been so mixed up about whether she was holding Sandy, so intent on keeping up a front, she honestly may not be able to distinguish between the real and the not real." His voice sharpened. "So how's my bargain?"

She said now he was the one playing detective.

"Not quite. You have a definite motive. You want to prove your brother didn't commit a murder. I just have this abstract interest. I want it for my information. My private bauble."

"Will you tell the police?"

"Private, I said," his flat voice insisted.

She kept her gaze on the intricacy of measured lines. "You've guessed something, I'm sure."

"I want it confirmed."

"To hold over my head?"

"I told you. Just the facts, ma'am."

She put out her hands. "Okay. It's true. I wanted to warn Sandy. David was making threatening noises, I didn't want anything to happen. But he didn't kill him," she went on in her tense voice. "He definitely did not. Do you believe me?"

"How should I know?"

"But—"

"You don't know for sure either. Otherwise you wouldn't be doing this."

Touché. She followed him into the next room, where more drawings were tacked to the walls. For a second his former voice impinged on her ear: this blueprint for a contest, this

we won, this we lost, this brought an unexpected bonus—
that running commentary that had catapulted them into instant friendliness. Different set of pictures here, different
circumstances.

With heavy deliberation, he went to a filing cabinet, took
out a couple of telephone bills, ran his finger down the
plainly delineated columns. March 10: Tulsa. March 11:
Chicago, Tulsa, Boston. March 12: Washington, D.C.—
mechanically, he read them out. This number he recognized: the group that was arranging that conference. This
one—just a second, he'd check it on their stationery—yes,
just as he thought: about the industrial park they were
working on in conjunction with another firm. This one,
well, hold on—another cabinet opened, another folder
consulted—friend of a friend of a client who wanted an ad-
dition to his house, turned out to be losing said house to the
bank. That left this number—could it be the supplier they
were trying for a special kind of black slate? Wait, he had
their stationery filed away too. No, not the supplier. So
maybe Margaret had hit pay dirt. Maybe not. He is making
no guarantees.

The Chicago number in question had been called four
times on a single day. 9:15 A.M., 10:30 A.M., 11:45 A.M., 5:10
P.M.—her gaze followed his finger down the computerized
column. Lovers' quarrel? Harsh words, followed by
harsher, then avowals of injured pride, to modulate, in the
mellow afternoon, into the tenderness of reconciliation? She
glanced at Ken—were they both assigning the same banal
interpretation to those uncommunicative numbers?

"Write it down if you want. Here's a pad." He started to
say something else, changed his mind, with his face slightly
averted, came out with it. "I have someone coming at two,
and this has taken so much time, afraid we'll have to cancel
that lunch date."

She nodded. Of course. She might have known. "Oh, my sweet mother, you really are deluding yourself"—Erica has it right again. Because what a delusion to think a man who is turned off by your playing the sly inquisitor will then turn around and welcome you as a favored lunch companion.

ELEVEN

MAYBE KEN was right. She shouldn't go to see that girl. As a project it was useless, meddlesome, intrusive, even, when looked at in a certain way, arrogant. She knew what facts she wanted to ascertain, but even if they should confirm her suspicions, would that constitute definitive proof? Would David thereby be acclaimed as innocent? The whole thing should be left, as Ken said, in the trained hands of the police, who in their bumbling way would come up with the answers.

By the time she worked around to these virtuous thoughts, however, she was in an aisle seat in a plane bound for Chicago, and she had an appointment that afternoon with someone called Leni Andrews. "A friend of Sandy's? Sure, why not. Come if you want," the voice after a pause had said on the phone.

She unfolded her newspaper. A flight she's taken often on business, and dressed as she is today: the gray suit, the high-heeled shoes, the capacious pocketbook. But it's what inside that brands you. Not your tailored outfit but your inner composure. The certitude that your errand has been thought out, approved through channels, arranged with certified goals in mind. That man sitting next to her—surely he can tell she's not a competent executive but a woman bent on going where she has no particular business?

But Leni Andrews wanted to talk—she said it as soon as Margaret walked in. She was longing to talk about Sandy. Now she knew what the books meant: Be in an uncertain position, and you can't wear your grief publicly, proudly. "I'll bet his wife isn't sitting alone. Oh, you don't have to

tell me, I can see from your face. Me, I couldn't even get off
from work. What can you tell them? My friend died? My
gentleman friend? My lover? They say they're sorry, but
they also quietly snicker.''

She sat primly, a pretty girl with small even features
framed by short dark hair. "You know how I heard? I called
the office yesterday. We had a code. I was the Andrews
Supply Company calling for Mr. Fleming—I think I sold
some fancy kind of kitchen tile. If it wasn't a good time for
us to talk, Sandy would say tell them I'll call back. So there
I was, nine-thirty in the morning to tell him I missed him or
loved him or whatever you say after a lonesome night, and
whoever answered, a fellow called Joe? He said Mr. Fleming is dead. Smack in the face like that, you get it. But he
was very nice. I was a business contact, wasn't I? You have
to be nice to business contacts. He told me everything. So
I've been sitting here like a zombie ever since. You have to
excuse the mess. Yesterday I found out my gentleman friend
is dead.''

"Oh, my dear, I'm sorry." She put her hand for a second
on Leni Andrews' knee. Actually, there wasn't much of a
mess, no more than you expect of a young woman's one-
room apartment. As for the young woman, she might feel
like a zombie, but what she looked was neat, compact, trim,
precise. The kind of image, Margaret thought, that someone whose heart had turned against Myra's blurry languor
would understandably go for. She would fit in to that uncompromising living room. Sitting with head upright, back
erect, she would add the definite note an architect's sensibility had in mind.

Her speech was definite too—quick phrases delivered in
a low husky voice. "Don't worry. I won't cry. Even though
I really did love him. How could you not? Any time he
opened his mouth, he sold himself. The way he could sell
anything. If he'd been selling pebbles, pebbles would turn
out to be the hottest item around. Well, what he was selling

were his own designs. Architectural designs. Am I talking
too much? Do you want me to stop? I have a friend who
wanted to buy a store to sell pottery, this silly sliver of a
place not even ten feet wide in some parts. She'd be crazy to
buy it, we all told her. But not Sandy. He explained how she
could make it work. A freestanding counter, and shelves lit
with pale purple or was it blue fluorescents, and curving
cabinets to follow the irregular wall—when he got through
describing it, you'd think that space was God's gift to
shopkeepers. And you know how he did it? A few little gestures, that's how. He waved his fingers and the ideas came
to life. A dream place, right there in thin air. No, I really am
not going to cry."

Margaret took off her jacket. The same terminology as
Myra, she thought: he sold you. Sandy Fleming, super
salesman. Of himself, of architectural plans, of ideas on the
way to live.

The girl gave a deep sigh. "Oh, I've needed this. To talk
and talk about him. I even thought about going to New
York, rounding up someone in his office. But you can't tell.
His partner, Kenneth Ash, isn't that his name? A wonderful man, Sandy always said, but suppose he's Myra's second cousin or something, he'd have to resent the person
Sandy was in love with. Even that Joe. He might be one of
those oddballs who thinks you should sleep only with your
own wife. You never know about people, do you? But now
with you here, I feel, how should I say it, liberated."

Liberation for me too, Margaret thought. This Leni Andrews obviously doesn't know about David. For the first
time since all this began, I'm not David's sister, not carrying around that ambiguous persona. I don't have to protest
his innocence or justify his ill will or defend the terms on
which he's chosen to live, I'm out of that particular bind.

"It's funny," Leni Andrews went on. "When Sandy was
alive I didn't feel the need to tell anyone. My New York
lover—he was my secret. Even at work—oh, I'm a dance

therapist—if someone wanted to get me a date, I just smiled that secret smile. It was part of the fun. Having Sandy all to myself. But now he's dead I have this yearning for everyone to know. I want a newspaper reporter to call up and interview me. I want to be a witness at the trial of his murderer. I want some architecture magazine to ask what I think of his latest work. Even his will. Does someone like Sandy leave a will? I want a lawyer to call and say there's this long paragraph about Leni Andrews.''

Margaret remembered how Myra, in moments of vehemence, would push the hair out of her eyes. This girl stood motionless; you can't in any case push hair that's cut short, in slanting bangs on a pretty forehead.

"Crazy," the girl said. "There's no way any of them could call me. Till last week I was just another of the girls he had affairs with. Oh, you don't have to deny it, he used to tell me himself. A whole string of them. But with me it was going to be different. Last week he asked me to marry him, he said now he could afford it.''

"Ah."

"His money worries were over, he said—isn't it ironic? That he had to die just when he was getting what he wanted." The girl picked up a bedspread from the floor and shook it. "Don't mind if I do a little housekeeping, do you? What he said was, he was coming into a bundle. It was just what he needed. Because he wanted to marry me, but he also wanted to treat his wife right. Leave her with something. That was Sandy." She fitted the spread over the edge of the daybed. "A really darling man.''

"Did you ask where this timely bundle was coming from?''

"We never went into that. I just thought, some great change in his business.''

Margaret was quiet a second. "He'd just deposited a hundred thousand dollars no one can account for. Would that be what he—''

The girl laughed. "A hundred thousand. Oh, you have to be kidding. No, he was talking about real money. Big money. Money for the way he liked to live." She picked up a skirt from the floor and hung it in the closet. "Listen. Once I took him to a cheap restaurant. We were on the way somewhere and it was raining and I said let's just go in here. Perfectly good food, but the bar was some cheap plastic and all around there was this tacky sort of nautical decoration. Fixtures like ships; lanterns, and anchors painted on the menus and table mats, and dingy fishnet draped over the walls. Nothing bad, honestly, but that man suffered. He left the food on his plate. He kept staring at the floor. He said he wasn't hungry. I mean, it really hurt him. Like every bit of cheap decoration was a stab at his heart."

She found a red sandal and then looked for its mate under the bed. "Even for me. I can't tell the difference, and still it had to be the best. See that fixture? Looks like any ordinary fixture, doesn't it? Big globe hanging from a skinny chain. Sandy bought it. I said one day that corner of the room was dark, and he said I'll get you something. Well, the chain was too long so I had to go to the store for them to fix it, and I saw the price. I wouldn't tell you. Nothing could make me. Family of four could live for a month on what that fixture cost. And you think a hundred thousand . . ."

For a moment she stopped working, she stood reflective. The pretty dance therapist with her effortlessly perfect posture. "Sort of a shame, really. That darling man, but money eating into him. Spoiling his fun. Well, why do I tell you. You knew him well, didn't you?"

"Yes." By now it's true. How can she not know him? You expect that the discarded wife and the loved mistress will come up with different appraisals: one starts from grievance, after all, one from tenderness—how can this not color what they see? But now she's got the line from Myra and Leni Andrews both: a man long on charm, short on cash.

Margaret watched as Leni resumed her housecleaning. Such a nice shrewd, competent girl, no wonder Sandy went for her. But the husky voice started again. "Don't be sorry for me."

"Okay."

"Should I tell you the truth? I hadn't decided about getting married. I wasn't sure. I loved him, that's right. But if you love someone, that doesn't mean...well, there was this dissatisfied side to him. All that big need for being rich, maybe it does something to you. And he never let up on it. He was always turning it over. The unfairness, he kept saying."

"Unfairness."

"That he didn't make more money. That's the way it was, he said. No matter how talented or creative an architect was, he never made as much as a lawyer. I don't know why, but that idea bugged him. It drove him up a wall. Oh, God, look at that sink. Would you mind if I washed some of those dishes?" But she didn't wash them. She stood still and shook her head. "I suppose I shouldn't talk like this. A man who's been dead only a couple of days. But it's the fact. I really had not made up my mind. So now I think if I'd been honest, it all would be different."

"Honest?"

"If I'd played straight. Told him right off I wasn't sure about getting married. Then he wouldn't have been so quick to give the news to his wife."

"Ah. When did he do that?"

"Before he left to come here," the girl said, and scraped something hard and yellow off a platter.

"You're sure of that."

"Positive. He figured it was the right thing to do. She took it very hard."

"I should think so." Margaret sat rigid. So all the time I was there, pressing her, saying which hotel and won't he call and when will you hear, during that whole tortuous session, Myra knew, she knew. This wasn't just any girl in the kind of series a wife can pretend not to notice; this was an announcement of the particular girl, the chosen one—no wonder I was treated to the sad little contradictions and the gaudy excuses and the cringing words like "unpredictable." There was no way Myra could get in touch with her husband, and my dumb questions just hammered in that unpalatable fact.

Then Margaret realized the import of what Leni had said. "But Myra couldn't have...I mean, she thought he was staying here till Saturday."

"Well, he decided to go back early. He had an idea for changing the wiring scheme in that house on Long Island, and he wanted to see the electrician before it got put in all wrong."

"Did Myra know he was coming home?"

"He called her from here. That phone on the desk. Called and told her his exact plans. He was worried about her. Worried about her state of mind. Isn't that a scream?" For the first time, the husky voice trembled. "Sandy being worried about how Myra felt. When all that time..."

"Listen. Do you think...are you saying that Myra killed him?"

The girl sat down, she put her head in her hands. "Naturally, I thought it. When I heard, I just took it for granted. After all, ten years of marriage, and then to hear she's on the way out. But now, when you ask me point blank like that." She raised her troubled face. "I don't know her. You do. You tell me. Is she the kind to kill someone?"

Margaret stood silent. Now I understand why I can't make the grade as a detective, she thought. Not because, as Ken insists, I can't round up clues as well as the police, and not because, as Erica fears, I'll land myself in trouble, but because I can't string along with the concept of murder. I have no feeling for it. I'm stone deaf to its nuances. I don't believe someone civilized—someone with whom I might in any way associate—would deliberately shoot another person. Oh, a crime of passion, sure, you go crazy when you see your beloved in a tangle with someone else on a bed, or blind instinct, you have to stop that madman from coming at you, or even canny self-protection, like that burglar hypothesized by Erica and Simon, someone with three offenses on his record who can't let himself in for a fourth. But to work up a study of possible schedules, and synchronize times, and wait with nervy patience for the apt moment, and meet the shocked bafflement in the gaze of a victim—I didn't believe it of my own brother, the truth is I can't believe it of anyone.

"... should have told him exactly how I felt. I was going to. But it always seemed the wrong time. I mean, when could I? Not on one of those faked-up phone calls, and not when he walked in all loving, and not..." Leni Andrews was still going on, that blend of grief and tenderness and self-reproof.

But Margaret interrupted. "Oh, my dear, just leave it alone. You're no more to blame for Sandy's death than I am."

TWELVE

ANOTHER DISCOURSE to herself on the way home. By right, she ought to feel great. She has found out who might have murdered Sandy. At least, she's found out who had a plausible reason for murdering Sandy. Means, motive, timing...it's all come together. The kind of comprehensible crime the police mentality can latch on to. The woman betrayed. And it lets David off the hook. If Myra killed her husband, David didn't. Q.E.D.

So why doesn't she feel better, as she sits in the plane going east? Why this hollow space in the pit of her stomach? Maybe that's why "triage" is such an ugly word, she thought. Choose one person to throw out of the sinking lifeboat, at the time it makes perfect sense, but the ones who are left feel guilt-ridden, craven, shamed, unworthy. Surely David will not like it. David, whose idea of the way to treat women has always been in the direction of courtliness, gallantry, even, if truth be told, chauvinism. He was proud of his sister's success in business but never quite reconciled to the idea of her being a businesswoman in the first place. If you and Erica need anything, you know I can swing it, he would say. So now to be saved at the expense of a woman's guilt—not to his liking at all.

And such a woman. Myra, who during her marriage surely saw the end coming but couldn't rouse herself to fight it by losing weight, or arranging her hair in some simple stylish way, or speaking out briskly, or impelling her body into firm and graceful poses. Sad-sack Myra, imagine. For her to be the one who took a gun, and made that long unnerving ride, and waited on that primitive driveway for Sandy to walk up...

Except suppose she didn't. Suppose, Margaret thought as she walked through the airport, it turns out that the woman betrayed had no chance of being on the spot. At noon of that critical day, she visited an art gallery. No, better than that. She was at a doctor's office, having a small cyst taken out of the side of her neck. The nurse will remember. Yes, Mrs. Fleming got a little faint, after the incision she had to lie down. Oh, yes, I did look in at her, I know the time because I had this lunch date but because we were so busy... It all is real: the overworked nurse and the cyst nestled in its small glass jar and the doctor gliding from room to room. Which one, Myra? Did you shoot your husband or were you lying on the doctor's leather couch—and getting into a taxi, Margaret heard herself give not her own address but Myra's.

In any case, she has her excuse. Twice she has gone to this house uninvited, but now she has her ticket of admittance, one to gain her instant entrance. Myra, that picture you offered me—if I could choose it now? Like saying you loved the book someone wrote, would like another portion of that casserole they cooked, of course want to see pictures of their grandchild. But for a second, she felt a qualm. Can she really do it? After ringing the door bell, to stand on that top step and give the message that says, in effect, I like your pictures? Praise for those blurry efforts with their arbitrary blobs of color and imperfectly thought-out compositions—won't Myra see right through her? Well, probably not. Sandy did it for ten years and got away with it. Well, maybe he didn't quite get away with it. "He didn't hang my pictures in here, there was that," Myra in a moment of pained candor had said. But on balance she had allowed herself to be taken in, that mechanism for self-delusion so necessary to any artist, that lets one dismiss the harsh truths while clinging to the expedient solace.

And in the end she didn't have to ring the bell. A woman was unlocking the door—after a moment, Margaret recognized her as Helene, the maid. A good sign. "Remember me? I was here a couple of days ago. You brought us tea."

Helene didn't immediately remember. She took her time, standing with her round rather expressionless face to one side, one hand on an ample hip while with the other she clutched her packages, before she gave the acknowledging nod. Well, that's a good sign too. A maid who doesn't let anyone in, checks and rechecks before issuing the welcoming words. Wait in here.

She waited in the showcase living room. In her mind—no, in her projection of Sandy's mind—it is now a room for Leni Andrews. That compact dancer's figure standing beside the mantel, the pretty face with the neat bangs held erect against the austere couch—it would satisfy whatever harmonious image he deeply cherished. It's an image that doesn't come easy. It takes time, work, attention, money. Mostly money. Money, she's found out, Sandy never had enough of, thought he was entitled to, held grudges when he couldn't acquire.

Oh, she's explored the man called Sandy Fleming these last few days, delved so far into his psyche that she can see a room through his demanding gaze. But she doesn't know Myra. Or at least she knows only the Myra who put her off with nervous deceit: I'll call him at the hotel, sometimes he changes his hotel, the hotel told me he moved out. If I concentrate on her paintings, Margaret thought, stand with her in that studio and focus on the works that are her main interest, will that do it? Will defensiveness give way to sincerity? There in the place where she puts in honest labor will she be more inclined to give honest answers?

But when footsteps sounded outside, it wasn't Myra. "You'd better come with me." Helene stood quietly at the door. Margaret started to answer, stopped, followed the broad hips through the hall, up the stairway, into the studio. The same route she once took with Myra.

And the same clutter. They are all still here. The marine landscapes, the lush flowers arranged against the contrasting geometric outlines of box or trellis, the repudiated abstracts, the palette on a table—light from that well-designed window streamed on all of it, so for an instant, only an instant, she didn't see what was just beside and under the table. She turned to Helene, but that woman stood motionless, obdurate against the wall, a caryatid in a blue cotton housedress. Okay, it's on me—she went over and bent down.

Are there tests for death? Tactics involving heart, pulse, color, breath? She doesn't know them, is not up to using them. But she knows Myra is dead. Here in her own studio, Myra has reached it at last: the ultimate in languor. Lying face down, feet slightly bent under the shapeless dress, hair disheveled on the floor, one hand spread out while the other has relinquished its grasp of a gun. There is even the requisite pool of blood beneath her—that deep red inexplicably tinged with green. Inexplicably till one sees the jar of green paint sideways on the table from which an intermittent drip still is falling.

Margaret turned. "My God. Dead, isn't she?"

"I guess so."

"Did you call the police?"

"I called you," the woman stolidly said, and Margaret suddenly appreciated the phenomenon. Me, I'd have yelled. A great bloodcurdling scream. Help! Help!—alerting neighbors, frightening passersby, doing no good at all. This woman had walked down and stood in the doorway and with no fuss, no hysteria, delivered her message: You better come with me.

"Where's the phone? Do you want to talk?" But Helene didn't, and Margaret was shortly the one at the kitchen table giving the salient facts. "Hurry! Oh, please hurry," she added, but the voice at the other end had already hung up, the wheels had presumably started turning.

"You don't look too good," Helene said. "Want some coffee?"

After what she'd seen, could she really drink coffee? Force it down? She sat at the table and found she could.

"Will the police come soon?" Helene wondered.

"They certainly should. Five minutes, maybe. But don't panic. Could be ten." Helene, however, shows no signs of panic. Amazing. Here I sit, still trembling, my heart wrenched into an irregular beat, my hand shaking so I've already spilled coffee on the table, while she stands there composed, her breathing even, her face wearing its expression of wooden calm. No emotion at all.

Maybe it's something in her background. Sandy found her in Bermuda and induced her to come to New York—wasn't that what Myra had said? Well, someone who would be willing to leave home and friends, come to a city where she has no ties—who knew what indoctrination in passivity, what years of detachment, might precede such a choice?

Or maybe it's something to do with the idiosyncrasies of temperament. We all respond differently to crisis. Tonight maybe she'll be the one to wake screaming, palms clammy, pillow drenched with sweat.

Margaret put down her cup. "Dear God. In her own studio."

"She was mostly there," Helene pragmatically said.

"She did love to paint, didn't she?"

"Did it all the time," Helene said.

Any other comments to make about Myra? Because this is the time to make them. Here they are, two middle-aged women in a kitchen, one sitting shakily at a table, the other standing levelheaded beside the stove while they pull out the rhetoric appropriate for the death of Myra Fleming.

Except not so appropriate if one of these women fancies herself a detective. Oh, Erica, right again. Shattered by the anomaly of death, here I sit forgetting my self-imposed function, wasting time, while the one person who knows most is allowed to remain silent.

She dabbed at the coffee stain. "Listen. Did you notice anything? I mean, how was she when you went out?"

Helene turned, as if she recognized the change of mode, but her voice continued toneless. When she went out, Mrs. Fleming had of course been fine.

"Were you out for long?"

"Three hours," Helene said and brushed a speck off the skirt of her housedress. "Three exactly. It was what she said. Go out for three hours."

"Mrs. Fleming told you to go out?"

"She said I should take in a movie. Or go shopping."

"When was this?"

"Two-thirty."

Margaret raised her eyes. In this well-ordered kitchen, the clock is exactly where one would expect it to be. Quarter to six.

"I did go to the movie but it wasn't good. I left after half an hour. I went shopping. I bought stockings and found the kind of garter belt I always want"—a faint blush: perhaps one doesn't mention a garter belt in company—"and I looked for a skirt but the stores around here are too expensive."

She's giving me an alibi. Thinks that's what's called for. "Oh, Helene—can I call you Helene?—nobody thinks . . . I mean, did Mrs. Fleming often do that? In the middle of a workday, tell you to go out?"

"She never did it before."

"But she did it today?" A waste. Three minutes gone by, and she is putting a question to which Helene has already given the answer. Well, then, why three hours? If Myra was planning to kill herself, why not send a maid home for the day? Did it really concern her that her body not languish on the inhospitable floor until, say, tomorrow morning? Or, on the other hand, if she didn't commit suicide, if she was the victim of someone who shot her and then arranged that gun to good effect, why did she want the house to herself for three hours? Was it for the sake of some visitor whose motives she sadly misjudged?

"Look. Did she seem troubled in any way this morning?"

"No more than usual," Helene tonelessly said. "Couldn't be too troubled or why would she want that meat?"

"What's that?"

"Over there. Yes, that package next to the sink. She called the butcher this morning. She said I should make her a stew, something to last for two days. She talked about it at lunch. A nice stew with mushrooms and baby onions. But if I was going to be out until half past five, no way I could get it ready before I left." Helene gave a judicial frown, one viewing a mystery strictly from the point of view of her own limited role in it.

Margaret looked again at the clock. If the police take only five minutes, they're parking outside this minute. No, double-parking. Police don't have to spend time edging into fortuitously vacant spots. If, however, they take ten minutes, she's the beneficiary of five minutes more. Five minutes in which to ascertain if there's anything significant this woman knows while not realizing that she knows it.

"So if she talked about the stew at lunch, she couldn't have been expecting to send you out. I mean, something came up. Something at the last minute."

"Must have," Helene neutrally agreed.

"Well, look. Did anything happen? Any upsetting phone calls? A violent argument that you maybe heard? A sudden phone call that bothered her? You're sure? Nothing at all?"

Helene shook her head, a noncommittal but resolute disclaimer. She once must have been pretty, Margaret thought. Good round eyes, a straight nose, approximation of rosebud mouth. Some faces age poorly—now the prettiness was buried in that fleshy impassivity.

"You mean she just—I want to get it straight—for no reason that you know of she decided you should go out for three hours?"

That was it, Helene said, and turned off the coffee maker.

A loud thumping noise outside. The police? No, from the sound of it a delivery truck asserting its rights over those of importunate drivers. Please hurry, she had said into the phone, but now she understands hurry is the last thing she wants. Let that call from headquarters to precinct house run into a mechanical snag. Let the first car they send out develop starter trouble. Let them meet with a mugging, a traffic accident on the way. You always hear about the hazardous delays when someone lies sick, tormented, but delays cannot hurt that woman lying upstairs.

"Oh, Helene, think. Try to remember. What happened before she told you about going out."

"Nothing. She saw her company to the door and then she came in here and told me."

"Company. Ah. Who was that?"

"A man."

Is she purposely being slow, doling out the facts one by one? No, her round face evinces no deceit, none of the sly pleasure of one who gets her kicks from teasing. "Was it someone you know?"

But Helene didn't. "He just turned up. Said he was an old friend of Mrs. Fleming's, and he'd read about the accident to Mr. Fleming, and since he was in the neighborhood he thought he'd pay a visit."

Margaret looked around the kitchen. Another showcase. In other circumstances, she would have her pencil out, taking notes. The faucets, the center island, the cabinets, the tile—all the stylish and workable items that just possibly might be integrated into some less dazzling scheme in her own kitchen.

"Helene, what about this old friend? What was his name?"

Another composed disclaimer. She didn't know. She didn't see him again. Not till Mrs. Fleming called her to the studio and asked her to wrap a picture for him to take home.

Oh, Myra. Someone more compliant than I was. You asked him did he want one, and he said sure, nice affable man. Just pointed and said that one—roses against a trellis? dawn over the mountain?—and made her happy. More than I could bring myself to do.

"But while you were in there she must have said something."

"Just that he was an old friend of her husband's, and they went to high school together, and he still lived in the same neighborhood where he used to then, think of that, and would I wrap this picture."

"But she mentioned his name? Or the place where he lived? Helene, that would be the natural thing—what's that noise! She'd have said, This is Mr. Soandso, and they went to school—oh, Helene, it's so logical."

She watched the expressionless features take this supposition, assess it, disavow it. Sorry. No name.

"Helene, what did he look like? I mean, was he extra tall, maybe? Extra short? Anything special?"

Helene shook her head. He was average height, it seemed. He had grayish brownish hair. He was wearing a regular business suit. Really, she didn't look closely.

Margaret pushed back her chair. Maybe if they talk briefly about something else. A conversation to disarm her, ease whatever tension is blocking the memory. She heard her sprightly tone. "Helene, you're from Bermuda, aren't you? Mrs. Fleming told me. I always wondered. It looks so beautiful, that place—are the pictures really true?"

"Yes."

"All those heavenly pink and white colors, and the beaches, and the sky. You must love it."

"Yes."

"I never went. I always wanted to, but somehow it was never the right time."

Silence.

"Which is the right time, would you say? I mean, for a tourist, which season is the best?"

"Good always for tourists."

Another failure. Helene is not getting disarmed, she's more distant than ever, lips pressed into two thin lines, eyes staring straight ahead. Well, hypnosis, how about that? You repeat in a monotonous tone the coercive words, till from its stubborn hiding place the crucial information is dredged up. Given the time, the conditions, she herself could do it.

There was no time. They were here now. Two policemen, and then two more, and then, from the footsteps going by in the hall, a small army. Those dispatched to the kitchen went in for solicitous pleasantries till word from the advance guard of the army came down: Myra Fleming dead all right, shot at close range through the heart, dead perhaps—though a precise estimate would have to wait for further tests—an hour and a half. That was all. Suicide? Murder? No way to tell from their circumspect tones what they thought, or even if they had a basis for thinking anything. And when two more policemen came down and started asking questions, these all related not to whatever untoward events in Helene's presence might have signaled the death, but to the hour and a half interval of her absence that had preceded it. Where during that time had Helene been? Well, then—pencils scribbling, paper rustling—what movie, which store? What about Margaret? She arrived at what time? Met Helene where? How long in the living room till she was informed about Mrs. Fleming's death? All the heavy facts capable of advancing the investigation, she thought, not one iota.

She looked at them, these officers working assiduously along the lines they were supposed to work. If they knew that the woman in the gray suit and high-heeled shoes was a competitor, that she was pushing ahead in her own way to solve a crime, would that alter their line of questioning? Would they then have the intuition, the cunning, to diverge from the prescribed text? Would they discern that the point calling for attention was not where a female domestic had gone on her time off but rather the motive that had prompted her employer, in what amounted to a drastic break with custom, to grant this time?

Helene stood dutifully next to the stove. Did she have her own ideas about what they should ask? Oh, who could tell what went on behind those composed features, the prohibitive gaze and the wooden voice, as she gave the answers to the next set of questions. Where she lived? An apartment near the East River on Ninety-first Street. How long she had worked here? Eight months. What were her hours? Ten to six. Duties? Cooking and cleaning. And meanwhile the crucial facts she possessed, if indeed she possessed them, were sinking deeper and deeper into the depths impervious to future questions.

THIRTEEN

THE PHONE RANG next morning before she was out of bed. "Mom, how about giving me advance notice next time?"

"Oh, Erica, honey...."

"I mean, it does give you a shock. You open the second section, you think you'll get the hot news on the strike of sanitation workers, and there is your own mother. Page 18, column 2. Mrs. Margaret Berringer, discoverer of the body."

"Erica, I was going to call the moment I—"

"Is this what happens when you go in for detecting? You have to be the first on the scene?"

That ironic tone, it's love and protectiveness and anger all at once. From across the wires, a sense of the girl's fresh loveliness came over her. Erica was sitting at her small table, Margaret thought. Drinking coffee and eating toast as she let loose this uncompromising tirade. On the other side of the room, the quilted cover had already been drawn up on the daybed—even as a child she had orderly habits. A natural for studio living.

"Erica, I was there only because Myra offered me a painting." The truth, isn't it? Or at least only a partial lie. "I refused it once, so—"

"That's why you went? You wanted one of her paintings?"

"I didn't exactly want it. Actually, they're not very good. But since I'd hurt her feelings that first time—"

"What about my feelings?" A crunching noise; Erica is polishing off the toast. "Honestly, Mom, how do you think I feel when you promise me you won't get involved, you say you're taking two weeks off from work just so you can give David support, and then there you are. In it up to your neck."

Did she promise not to get involved? "Just because I happened to step into that house at half past five..."

"I'm talking about the whole day. Eight hours of being incommunicado. When David needed you and couldn't get you. Some support."

"Oh, God, did something happen?"

"Calm down. It's okay. We handled it."

She sat rigid on the edge of the bed.

"Mom, where were you from nine o'clock on? If you weren't, as you say, with Myra, and you weren't at home or at your office?"

Her mind's eye presented her with that stern, fair, authoritarian face. This is what they write about: role reversal, the daughter, out of her impressive experience and superior prowess, being the one in a position to lay down sanctions and make judgments and insist on safeguards. She'd known it was coming, of course; she'd envisioned it as a cozy appurtenance of some misty future, but here it is being ushered in when she's forty-six and Erica twenty-four. Well, there's something comforting about it, no question.

Comforting and also, under the circumstances, inconvenient. "Yesterday was no big deal. I just—" Just took a plane to Chicago and back. She coughed. "Tell me what's with David?"

"His man, what's his name? Lawrence? He threatened to walk out. There was a row. Something about David spying on Lawrence, checking up—sounded wild, I couldn't understand it."

I can. "I'll go right over."

"Mom, listen. Tell me it's finished. I mean, there's no reason anymore, is there? Myra killed herself, isn't that the idea? And even if she didn't, David couldn't have done it, a studio room three flights up, the paper said. So if he didn't kill Myra Fleming...Mom, are you listening? Will you give it up? Will you?"

"Yes." Another lie. "Erica, honey, I have to run."

A panicked run. Ever since the accident, the same nightmare has hung over her. David blurts out some of his provocative remarks, whoever is taking care of him walks out in a huff, David is alone. Man at the mercy of his incapacitating affliction. Sometimes when they tell her at work the phone is for her, her hand trembles when she picks it up, she knows what she will hear: Maggie, can you get over here right away?

But when she walked in, breakfast was on the tray of his wheelchair; sun shone through the slats of the venetian blinds; the sound of washing came from the kitchen; David was dapper in a blue sport jacket. "Maggie, love, sit down. You want coffee? No, first tell me everything. What is all this? Myra Fleming dead? You actually found her?"

She told him briefly.

"How come you went over there?"

She looked up sharply. Another session like the one with Erica, with her being pushed into some defensive, placating, vaguely meretricious position? No, thank heavens, it has evidently not occurred to David that his sister has any but the most superficial involvement. He accepts her story about the painting, makes the requisite comments about Myra, even lets her lead him into a few subdued remarks about Sandy, at which point it is appropriate for her to put her question: Does he happen to know where Sandy grew up and went to high school; did Sandy ever mention that when they were working together?

"He did mention it. Westport, Connecticut. I think there was plenty of money in his family.... Maggie, why do you ask?"

"No reason." She took a piece of toast from his tray and asked what the problem had been yesterday.

"I was trying to find out about Lawrence and—well, you know. Probing, probing." His voice sank to a whisper. "Guess I'm not such a good detective."

You and me both, Davey.

"Questions about which bar he goes to when he's out and whether it has a TV—you can see how they'd be misunderstood. He thought I was curtailing his free time or implying that he shouldn't have free time or just poking my nose into what was none of my business—he said things he didn't mean, I said things I didn't mean...."

"David, will he stay on?"

"You don't have to whisper. It's all cleared up. We worked it out. Lawrence? Oh, Lawrence, I told Mrs. Berringer everything's shipshape between us."

Like a marriage, she thought again, seeing the courteous bow from Lawrence answered in the gratified nod from David. Patient and nurse: dependence holds them, inescapable closeness defines them. The great emotional swings, the capacity to inflict damage, the arguments that paint one into a corner, the pain on both sides if there is a break-up...a ritualized union, bound by contract, recognized by statute.

"The truth is, it really was touch and go for a while," he said after Lawrence went out. "There I was, wanting to know about who told the police, and there he was, starting to gripe about hours and pay and vacation and work. I was furious. If that's what he thought of the job, he could clear the hell out. But then I noticed this rash on my arm. Here!— well, it's just about gone now. I thought it might be that new medicine. You know, the muscle relaxant, the doctor said there might be some side effect. But then if I changed, went back to Robaxin, it might be something else entirely, the Colace, say, or the Hiprex, and in any case that long period of adjusting and measuring and trying to figure out by trial and error which is the culprit...no time to be switching nurses."

Saved by the hypochondriacal instincts! "Obsessive preoccupation with body and its anatomic functional impairment"—that was how one of the doctors had characterized David in the early days after the accident. Well, right now she is grateful for that obsession, both of them, at this difficult time, can focus on it, cling to it, draw from it the safe conversational sustenance.

"I passed that new produce store on the way here. A block further than the old, but it looks as if they have better stuff. Why don't I mention it to Lawrence?"

He nodded. She should do that.

"I was thinking. If you'd have your green vegetable at dinner, along with something light like maybe cottage cheese, and keep the meat for lunch..."

Another nod. Sounded a good plan.

"No big change, but it might help the problem of—David, what are you writing?"

"Just scribbling the theories this new death must have introduced."

She put out her hands: all right, the obsession won't hold them. "Theories like what?"

"Well, who killed whom. As I see it, there are now four possibilities. No, five. Myra killed her husband and then using another gun—they did say a different gun in the papers, didn't they?—she took her own life. Someone else killed Sandy and Myra took her own life. The same person killed Myra and Sandy. I killed Sandy and—"

"David!"

"Just reviewing what I have no doubt the detectives are thinking," he said flatly. "I killed Sandy and someone else came in and killed Myra."

She looked up. Bitterness in that flat tone? Irony? No, actually a perverse kind of relish. It's a relish that troubles her. The publicity, the attention, the fact of being in the public eye—he likes it, Erica astutely said two days ago. Today that liking seems to her feverish, almost manic. She studied her brother, in his blue jacket with the nautical gold buttons. What does it mean that he keeps coming back with pained irony to this subject, that he insists on mention of himself as a suspect? If he's flying so high now, is he letting himself in for a wounding descent? Is there some moderating element she can interject? .

In the end she drank the coffee Lawrence brought and then said she had to leave.

"Going shopping, Maggie?" David asked.

She kissed him and went out in the cool sunlight. Shopping—ha! Shopping for a man without name or address, a man of medium height, average looks, brownish grayish hair, no distinguishing characteristics. A man of whom she knows only that he may live in Westport, Connecticut, where twenty-five years ago he went to school with Sandy Fleming, and that yesterday afternoon he paid a visit to Sandy's wife.

She walked down Park and then switched to Madison, where there was more interest. Windows full of hand-loomed sweaters, antique jewelry, high-priced lingerie, confident paintings. Window after window full of paintings—incredible. More incredible when one thinks that for every artist who has made his way in an ornate frame into one of these mannered settings there are thousands like Myra whose paintings make it out of the house only in the shape of forced bequests to obliging guests. Did he carry his picture home on the train, that complaisant man? Did his wife say, My God, where'd you ever get that thing! Did he say it might not look too bad in their downstairs play-room? Margaret stopped; she stood frozen on a corner, ignoring the changing lights, while a man carrying a plant circled past, and two young women pushing baby carriages, and a boy trundling a hand truck who said, Watch it, lady. Then she hailed a taxi because she knew how she was going to find him, her undiscovered Mr. Average.

At Grand Central she had just missed a train—an hour till another. She didn't mind. Time to think, after her nervy decision. Should she call the police, let them in on her plans? But as she walked over to the newsstand, she felt an obscure defiance. They're not letting her into their deliberations. Here she is, able, willing, and she doesn't know the most elementary facts. By reason of simple logistics, David is a candidate for Sandy's murder, but what about the other principals? Where were Ken or Simon between twelve and three on the crucial day? Do both of them have watertight alibis? Does one of them? This is something the police must surely have checked, but no one has felt it necessary to confide in her.

Besides, they had the same opportunity she did; they were privy, there in Myra's kitchen, to the same cryptic pieces of information from Helene. If theirs is such a skilled and efficient organization, as Ken says, why don't they think of this scheme themselves?

No, as she walked under the vaulted ceiling, the real quiver in her heart had to do with Erica. Suppose Erica should walk by this minute and see her mother, in direct contravention of orders, in the small knot of people waiting to board a train to Westport. At ten-thirty in the morning there is no chance of Erica walking through the upper level of Grand Central Station, but still the portent is there: role reversal with a vengeance. This is how young adolescents must feel, she thought. Does Mama somehow know I'm kissing this boy, having this drink, smoking this cigarette, cutting this class—that consciousness of being always exposed, subject to some awesome parental surveillance.

Well, no one spotted her. Not when she followed the knot of people down the grimy stairs, not when she chose a window seat on the train, not when she got out at the station and asked a taxi to take her to the office of the local newspaper. Then, for a moment, as she stood on one side of a high counter, a sinking heart. Sure, she can put in an ad, the man on the other side of the counter told her. What size? Big as she likes. Let's see her layout.

"Layout."

"We have to know what you have in mind."

"I don't have—I mean, I just know what I want to say."

"Come back when you have it set up," he told her.

She moved aside while a woman in a green pants suit swept in, handed over a page of copy topped by a picture of a house, said run it for three days, swept out. Lucky woman, all she wants is to get half a million for her waterfront property. Then Margaret looked at her interlocutor. Not a man at all, just a kid with red hair, scarred face, dirty fingernails.

"Listen. Is there someone in the, um, layout department who might be willing to help me? I'd be willing to—I mean, it's important."

The look of puerile sternness went over her. Then he said, Wait a minute, Manny might just have the time.

At least Manny was older. Older, bearded, cooperative. Too cooperative: he thought courtesy demanded that he give her options. What was her preference in type style, and caps or lowercase letters, and how much space between the lines, and how about a little attention-getting design in the borders? She sighed, sitting next to him on the small bench. "Manny, you design it, please. Yes, that looks great. No, really, I want it just like that."

Finished? Not quite. She has to decide how large an ad. A full page? Half a page? Quarter? Eighth? How to strike a happy medium? Something that will be noticed but at the same time won't look suspicious, so people think who is this nut? In the end they agreed, she and the well-intentioned Manny. An eighth of a page to run for a week and bearing four simple lines: COLLECTOR INTERESTED IN PURCHASING PAINTINGS BY MYRA FLEMING. HIGHEST PRICES PAID. CALL—and her number. Now comes the hardest part, which is to sit by the phone and wait.

FOURTEEN

THE WAITING BEGAN at five o'clock the next afternoon. Five—surely the hour at which local papers are delivered? Margaret closed her eyes and the scene took shape. Mr. Average works in the city and doesn't get home until seven— ah, those hard-pressed suburban husbands—but in the few minutes after his wife has put the roast in the oven and before she goes upstairs to help the oldest child with his algebra homework, she has time to pick up the paper from the porch and sneak a quick look—then she tears out the crucial page to show her husband at dinner. If he has a wife. And if she is not on that commuter train with him. And if he brought the painting home instead of chucking it into the nearest trash can.

Well, at least she knows that women who live in places like Westport do read local papers—she can still hear the voice of the friend who twenty years ago was petitioning her to move to the country. "I'll send you a list of houses from our local paper. Well, sure we have one, Mag—how could we live without it? How else would we know who was getting a divorce and what store was broken into and whose son lost his license for the second time for speeding? It's indispensable, it has absolutely all you want to know. Move up here, Maggie darling, and you won't ever have to read another thing."

How long is she going to sit here, rigid, vigilant, waiting for some call that may never come? When she called David an hour ago, she sighed purposefully and said she felt a bad headache coming on, maybe no visit today. Which leaves her free to wait for one whole day anyhow. If there is no answer by tonight, she can parlay that putative headache into an incipient grippe—another couple of days gained.

Or she can simply leave the house and go about her business. No reason she has to be a captive. She can leave and trust that if Myra's obliging visitor calls up and gets no answer he will call back; an unanswered phone will not reinforce his conviction that it was all a joke in questionable taste.

Or she might install a message: "If you are calling in regard to the purchase of Myra Fleming's painting, please leave your name and telephone number and I will return your call as soon as possible." But suppose David calls. Or Erica, and hears what she will consider this betrayal by her mother? Or Ken. No, not Ken. He must have read this morning's paper, he now knows that to the obliquity of having asked unsuitable questions in his office has been added the blunder of having discovered Myra's body.... No, Ken Ash will not be making calls of casual friendliness to this phone.

So she must sit here. Well, she's an old hand at waiting. Is the tumor malignant or benign, will it be a girl or a boy, will the college of her choice admit her or not—by the time you're forty-six, you've put in your time waiting for the answers. But in these cases, there are always time limits. By next Tuesday or tomorrow noon or the middle of April the outcome will be known. It may not be the outcome desired, but an outcome nonetheless. Suspense ended.

But how endure a period that is open-ended? That may terminate in a day and may stretch on for a week and may never achieve any result at all. Worse, how endure it in a place not set up for purposeful activity? She's always prided herself on having cultivated a certain stoicism during these periods, an ability to go ahead with life, as if this were a test of moral fiber. You don't sit around waiting. If the doctor's office says call at five, at three-thirty you embark on a report, start a new project, call the staff in for a meeting. But moral fiber in her own apartment! Margaret Berringer, who leaves every morning at eight in her tailored suits, who has never gone in for housekeeping, who has no aptitude for hemming curtains or laying scalloped paper on shelves, how long is she willing to give to this ludicrous, uncertain, possibly fruitless enterprise?

And what if by having made herself a sitting duck by staying home, it's the wrong person on the telephone? It was the wrong person at ten o'clock next morning. "Maggie?"

"Oh. Alex." Trust an ex-husband to turn up.

"Maggie, darling, how terrible for you, why didn't someone tell me?"

"Alex?"

"I've been away, a business trip. I just got back last night and I saw the papers."

"I sort of wondered why you didn't call," she said truthfully.

"Maggie, you all right?"

Yes. Sure. Fine.

"I called your office first thing."

What excuse had she given for not going in? "Oh, well, some work at home," she murmured.

"I don't blame you if you feel shitty."

Another murmur: she does feel shitty, why shouldn't he think so?

"David, how's he doing?"

"Well, you know. Bearing up." Her tongue felt thick; there were no signposts; how did one thread one's way through this conversation?

"God, what a lousy thing. If I could do anything, anything at all."

"Alex, we really know that."

"Maggie, awful to be so out of touch. Before we talk about David, tell me about yourself. I ask Erica, but that scrupulous girl, you know how close-mouthed."

She did know. Erica had an uneasy relationship with her father that both of them worked at with intelligent purposefulness: lunches, dinners, once in a while a weekend. After these occasions, Margaret often felt and always resisted the impulse to pump her. Tell me about him. How's his life? Does he have a woman? And Erica, for her part, divulged nothing.

She said there was nothing for Erica to tell.

"No...man?" He said it in a tone that to her denoted sweetness and anxiety both. Oh, well, a marriage never really ends.

"No man. Not really."

"I've been dating," he said in a morose voice. "Sometimes it's not too bad." A long pause. "Maggie, listen. I wasn't on a business trip, I was on a cruise with this woman. Someone very snappy and good-looking and nice. And you know what? I don't care if I never see her again. Six days with all that hoopla, and I kept comparing her to you, and she didn't measure up. That's the God's honest truth."

Is it? Or has the occasion swept him away into self-delusion? Doesn't matter: she can use a little of that kind of talk now.

"Maggie, baby, why don't we have lunch?"

"I have to stay here." I'm waiting for another phone call.

"You said you weren't sick."

"I just have to stay in the apartment, someone, um, coming to measure the windows."

Another pause, then he said, okay, he'd bring lunch to her. One of those gala picnic baskets they put up at the place on the corner. A still more meaningful pause, his voice lowered; across the phone she could see the look of ruefulness on his face. "Maggie, remember when we were supposed to meet the Blakes in the park, we had the picnic all ready, wine, lemon chicken, the works, and we told them..."

Of course she remembers; how can she not remember? He said why don't we stay home all day, and they did stay home, the lovemaking enhanced by the fact of all the eager friendships and glorious weather and brisk activities over which it was taking precedence. She twisted the spirals of the telephone cord. What's going on here!

Well, she knows what's going on, and she likes it. Or at least she doesn't not like it. For a man to wish to give amorous comfort to an ex-wife at a time of grave trouble—not customary, maybe, but certainly not wrong. And who is in a better position than he? For twenty-five years he made a study of what was warm and soft and vulnerable about her; he was the world's leading expert on the subject. Oh, it's what she needs, what she's longing for.

"Besides, I really want to make sure David is doing the right thing by himself."

"Right thing?"

"In terms of a lawyer."

She sat down. "Alex, things aren't at all at that state."

"But he should be thinking about it. Rounding up the proper person. Of course he knows plenty of lawyers from his work. Good solid pin-striped corporate types. The kind that never get their hands dirty with anything messier than a gold-plated merger. But he's going to need someone very different with this. Someone who understands—"

"Alex, what are you talking about?"

"Criminal lawyers. The kind who know all the tricks. How to pick the jury. How to con the jury. How to coach David so he gets every ounce of sympathy that's coming to him and still doesn't—"

"You're taking for granted there's going to be a trial."

"Hell, Maggie, I've been at this all morning, I had the back issues of every paper brought in; from what I read there's not a chance he—"

"Maybe you read wrong."

"Come on, Maggie, who's kidding who? This is Alex you're talking to."

"Listen. David did not kill Sandy."

"Maggie, baby, I know how you feel. Believe me, my heart is with you. David! Our David! Obviously it strains plausibility. Well, let me tell you about the case in Boston last year. Burglaries in an upper-crust community. They started in parking lots where women were at meetings. P.T.A.'s, League of Women Voters—like that. The fellow would park in some remote corner of the lot, and when a woman came out, without getting out of his own car he'd hold a gun on her. Then he graduated to houses. Strictly first-floor operations. Suspicion pointed to a certain paraplegic, but people said that was crazy, someone like that would never, until it was discovered that in fact—"

"Alex, David *did not kill Sandy*."

"Besides, it's not really fair to judge him by normal standards. Shall I tell you something? After the accident I myself had fantasies of doing something to Sandy. Oh, not murder, of course, but something to ruin his reputation, blast him out of the profession . . ."

"Alex, I have to go now."

She was still trembling when the next phone call came. "Hello?" The indecisive hello of someone who isn't sure what he's getting into. But she let him talk on, a pleasant, slightly hoarse male voice, about having read an ad in last night's paper and feeling puzzled, thinking it might be a joke.

"Not a joke at all, I assure you."

A trap, then, he said. Though who would be trapping whom and why he can't imagine.

"Oh, surely not a trap. Look. My name is Margaret Berringer." Then she told him where she worked and where she lived.

"Well, mine's Lester Sommers. And I do in fact have a picture by Myra Fleming."

"Mr. Sommers, that's wonderful."

"I suppose you want to know what kind of picture it is."

Well, no, that wasn't really—

"A landscape," he said with his hoarse determination. "Three or four small fishing boats, and some indistinct figures in the distance."

"Mr. Sommers, I'd very much like to see your picture. If it's a genuine Myra Fleming."

His voice was wry. No problem about that.

"Perhaps I could come up to Westport?"

He answered briskly, that obliging Mr. Sommers. That wouldn't be necessary. Actually, having read the ad last night, he had brought the picture to his office this morning. He gave her the address: an accounting firm on Seventh Avenue near Twenty-eighth Street—how did three o'clock this afternoon sound?

You always worry if things come too easy. All this agreeable talk, but maybe he sees it as a chance to extort real money. Should she mention a price now? How high is she prepared to go? And suppose she pays out money and then hears that he's unwilling to talk? Should she inform him at the start there's a quid pro quo?

In the end the decisions were taken out of her hand. He met her at the door of his office and escorted her into a room furnished with heavy leather furniture and a massive table, and he said, "Mrs. Berringer—it is Berringer, isn't it?—well, then, am I right in thinking you're after something more than the painting of a dead woman?"

She sat down. Outmaneuvered. But then she looked at him, this man who was not tall and not short, not thin and not fat, but just as Helene had said, an average man in an ordinary business suit, and she saw there was nothing ominous about his face. "That's right. I really did want to know who you were."

He sneezed. "Excuse me. I seem to be getting a cold." Then he said it was a very clever scheme.

"It seemed obvious, once I thought about it."

"Well, so you found me. But I can't imagine why you'd want to."

"Oh. Well, you visited Myra Fleming a couple of hours before she died, maybe you were the last person to visit her...."

He sat opposite her. "Mrs. Berringer, I think we ought to get some things straight. I have nothing to hide, I'm glad to answer any questions, but if you're from the police I'd like to know about it."

Easy to be honest about this one. The visit was personal, she said.

"Anything to do with insurance, then?"

"You mean, because she may have committed suicide? Mr. Sommers, I'd better come clean. My brother David is a suspect in the murder of Myra's husband Sandy—maybe you read his name in the papers. So it's really important to me to find out all I can about Sandy and Myra."

"You mean, you're constituting yourself an unofficial detective?"

She looked at him quickly. No malice. Just the predictable inflamed nostrils and red-rimmed eyes. She said unofficial about described it.

"Well, then, Mrs. Berringer, I have to tell you you'd be wasting your money. Sandy and I were high school friends. I hadn't seen him for twenty-five years. There's nothing I can tell you that—Oh, excuse me."

She waited till this set of sneezes was finished. Then hurriedly, before her own qualms could make her change her mind, she said she would pay him five hundred dollars for the painting.

"You're a determined woman, aren't you? Maybe you'd better look at it first."

It was in a corner of the room, propped up against one of the large leather chairs, and the wrapping was not very neat—after he opened it to show that vigilant wife, he didn't do as good a job as Helene must have done the first time. But Myra's painting, all right: the blurred sky, the inept boats, the man and woman in raincoats on shore for no reason demanded by artistry or composition except that at some moment when she stood at her easel the thought of a couple in rain gear must have entered Myra's head.

"There you are. You can still say no. I wouldn't blame you. Unless you're really interested in scenes of boats," he added with no irony.

But she already had her checkbook out. Someday I'll tell David about this and he'll pay me, she thought.

"Mrs. Fleming didn't say anything important," he went on doggedly, through his stuffed nose. "Surely not about being depressed or I wouldn't have left her. She was just a woman whose husband was dead." As if in apology for having taken her check, he sneezed again: a man who looked average and had an average cold.

"Maybe you said something. About Sandy," Margaret prodded.

"I couldn't have. I told you—high school classmates. His family moved away when we were seniors and I never saw any of them again." He put out his hands: Look, ma'am, no facts.

All at once she felt so tired she could hardly speak. Why is she doing this? What can she possibly expect to find out? She's thrown away five hundred dollars—isn't it time to cut her losses? She heard her voice as if it were an independent organ asking him to tell her anything they talked about, he and Myra.

"Old times. What else could there be? I was there to pay a condolence call, so I told her about the Sandy I knew." His voice was brisk; as her spirits went down, his had risen. "When Sandy was sixteen. Seventeen. Going on eighteen. Mrs. Berringer, wouldn't you be more comfortable in this chair?" His chair was a swivel, and he twirled gently in it. "Funny about high school," he said in his hoarse eager voice. "No other time of your life is ever so vivid. Maybe it's something to do with your stage of growing up. By college you've made the break from parents, you know who you are, you can concentrate on books. But high school...everything counts. Every moment full of significance. You hate your parents and you love them, you trust your friends and you know they're out to cut your throat, you're in awe of your teachers and you go in for snide speculation about their sex lives...everything magnified. I don't even remember my dorm room at college, but high school! Ask me anything. Where did I sit in math? Which dress of the Spanish teacher let us look down her front? What girl's hand did I hold sitting in the back of Simon Fleming's car? It's all there. Sharp. Is that the way it is for girls too? Every detail engraved forever?"

She leaned back in the leather chair. He's enjoying this. She's tapped that vein of nostalgia that lies deep in every man. While he sits in this pompous room dispensing advice about tax shelters and deductibles, this is what he would like to be talking about: his high school days. So now he has it: a therapeutic session, except he has been paid for having it. His reddened eyes look out warmly, though not exactly at her: what he's seeing is the view down the Spanish teacher's dress.

Mr. Sommers blew his nose. "Sandy and Simon Fleming," he said. "Every once in a while I've wondered what happened to them. Sandy got to be an architect, of course, I read that in the paper, but Simon, did I hear he was a lawyer?"

"Very successful one," she said.

"Well. Doesn't always happen like that. The ones who were whiz bangs at school, years later you hear about them, they're running health-food stores in some mountain village, or trying to make a go of a used-car lot. So the Fleming boys both made it. Well, well. Because they were sure enough the big boys then. Popular, we called it. I have a daughter in high school now, she says they don't use the word anymore. Old-fashioned. But what else do you say about someone who's Mr. Big? All the girls are in love with him and the boys think he's hot stuff too. Right in there. I mean, hanging around with Sandy and Simon, that was the place to be." Another onslaught on his suffering nose. "And I really mean place. The Fleming house. The Fleming car. Even the Fleming boat. And it wasn't just money. Lots of Westport families in those days were in the chips. But they didn't do what the Fleming parents did. Give their kids a car for use round the clock. Have a kitchen stocked at all times with sandwiches and beer. Make their living room available any time some adolescents are out for a high old time—Mrs. Berringer, am I talking too much? Just say so."

She can't say anything. She feels numb. Imagine: she thought she might have trouble getting him to talk, this man whose high school days lie close to his heart. He can't talk about them to anyone else. Not that again, Les, his wife tells him. Oh, Daddy! his daughter dismissively says. But here he is with a woman who asked for it, schemed for it, constituted herself a captive audience. He can churn up that great wave of his past, and she can't claw her way out. She has to sit still. Her job is to remain alert, interested, bound by the dubious theory that in any voluminous flood a significant speck may turn up.

She asked wanly if this was what he had talked about to Myra.

"What else was there? Like I said, I remember every detail. The good old days. Almost like a biblical era. So when they ended you sort of figured that was the end of the world."

Someone stuck his head in, said, Oh, excuse me, backed out. "You mean at graduation?"

"Actually, they ended before that. Don't ask me why—just good times finished. I couldn't enlighten Myra either," he added through a wad of Kleenex, "so don't ask."

She indicated by her upright posture that she was asking.

"A puzzle, that's all," he said. "Suddenly the Fleming house isn't available. The Fleming car is reserved for Papa, even though he has two other cars of his own. The Fleming boat stays at the dock. Even the Fleming lawn where we used to have pick-up football games—uh uh." Another morose blow on his nose; they feed on each other: lament for that thwarted past, pain for the current ills. "And the Fleming boys, where are they? Home by ten, that's where. New rules. Strict curfew. Fun finished."

"I don't understand."

"Neither did I. Neither did any of us. All of a sudden, a new regime."

"Just like that, it happened?"

"Just like that. They'd been away someplace for spring vacation. Bermuda? I guess, that's where they used to go—they were the kind of family who took vacations together. Anyhow, quiet as hell without them, when Simon and Sandy come back things'll pick up was what we said. Except this time they didn't."

"If Sandy was your friend, didn't you ask him?"

"High school friends—you don't ask questions. You jockey for position. If you're in the crowd, you figure what can you do to stay there. Anyhow, that's how it was twenty-five years ago. To hear my daughter I don't think it's so different now." He fumbled in his pocket for more Kleenex. "All we knew, the party was over. Know that book, *The Great Gatsby*? Our class was reading it then. That great blazing house, only suddenly the lights go out? It was like that."

She had to smile. *The Great Gatsby* quoted in this room where the leather-bound volumes—Tax Codes of 1956, Tax Codes of 1957, Tax Codes of 1958, years and years of them in solemn brown—enveloped the walls. "Someone must have said something."

"We had plenty of theories. It wasn't marks, either of them flunking out. Simon went off to whatever Ivy League college had given him the nod, and Sandy, he was okay too.

Not up on top of the class, never that, but okay. We thought for a while business reverses, old man Fleming lost his money, or someone suing his pharmaceutical company for deformed children, we were big on that idea, but nothing like it ever came out. So we figured private family business. The mother was a beauty, about twenty years younger than the father; we decided maybe she was running around and he took it out on the kids. Or maybe just a regular break-up between them. Or maybe menopause. We didn't know exactly what it meant but we thought it was a classy word and we used it. Male menopause, to signify an old man's crochets. Someone clamping down on his kids."

Mr. Sommers started wrapping the picture, smoothing out the brown paper, pulling at the inadequate string. "We always thought the hard feelings between the boys dated from around then. They weren't true brothers—I guess you know that. Simon was adopted. No one had thought much about it before, they'd just been the usual adolescents, some blowups but on the whole good feeling. But after that there was... I don't know how to say it. Something edgy. Competitive. They needled each other. Seemed to get on each other's nerves. Maybe it always has to be like that. Parents can't fall apart without its taking a toll on the kids. I know in my family—well, you didn't pay five hundred dollars to hear about me." He stood up: session over.

"That's all you told Myra?"

That was all. Sorry. Then he gave his watery smile. "Hope you got what you wanted."

Such a nice humorless man. So confiding, so earnest. "It was a big help," she lied. "Thank you very much." She started for the door, but he stopped her.

"Hold it, Mrs. Berringer. You forgot to take your picture."

FIFTEEN

"HOWEVER, THE PAINTINGS remain, a legacy of great variety and wonderful dexterity. So in a sense, although she is dead, we cannot really say..."

Margaret leaned forward on the wooden bench. The minister obviously did not know Myra, and at first she felt the spasm of anger that is inevitable when something as solemn as death is tainted by falsity. Then she reconsidered. It was probably just as well: the whole enameled oration false. About Myra as a fulfilled woman, and about the dextrous paintings, and also about the manner of her death. Not being under the obligation to say anything personal, he could skate gracefully past it. In his script, she was just a woman who happened to die in her forty-second year.

"There is a verse from one of the psalms..."

He had a good resonant voice, though in fact resonance was hardly needed. There were not many for it to reach, in this room that was surely the smallest in the funeral chapel. Simon and his wife in the front row, along with two women she didn't know. Ken and another couple in the row behind them, then a couple of empty rows, then, toward the back, Margaret, and beside her a woman in a handsome green suit, green shoes, a small green pillbox hat. Then a few scattered behind—no more than twenty in all.

"You were sweet to come," a woman had said at the door, but she also looked surreptitiously at a list, as if to make sure Margaret was really among the desired guests. For a second Margaret was also baffled. This serenely attractive woman with tendrils of hair around her heart-shaped face—hadn't she seen her someplace before? Then the soft voice went on, "Simon is inside, he'll be glad to see you," and she knew. Dianne. That wife who would always do everything right, be at his side when needed, disappear when that was called for.

And in fact Simon had not been inside, or at least he had not been visible until the doors were closed and the service began. It was Ken who saw her after she walked down the aisle and slipped in next to this woman in green. Saw her and gave her a curt, unfriendly nod. Or was she imagining it? One isn't expected to go in for cheery greetings at a funeral, but surely in that abbreviated glance he could have displayed more cordiality.

"Death at such a remarkably early age..." the minister said, and Margaret stiffened. Now a look at some of the unsavory details? No, he was too practiced for that. Especially since these details hadn't yet been satisfactorily established. Suicide? Murder? This morning the papers quoted a detective as saying cryptically that while suicide seemed an obvious bet, a gun positioned accurately next to someone's hand did not always mean what it appeared to mean. Margaret turned slightly, looking for the woman who also saw that gun. That stolid Helene, where is she? Curious. Surely the domestic turns up, a fixture of every funeral, sitting toward the back in her unaccustomed black dress, her emphatic hat, her showy gloves. "She was a gem," one of the old friends whispers to another. "Wonder if she's looking for another job," the friend craftily whispers back.

But no Helene—can it be that the distant look on her face was really a measure of some inner unconcern? No police either, unless that man in a dark suit toward the door is a detective counting noses.

"...and to those who mourn her, her brother-in-law and sister-in-law, her cousins, I say that..."

So those women sitting in proprietary fashion next to Simon and Dianne were cousins. When she turned, the woman in green was also observing them. "He did the best he could with meager materials," the woman said as the resonant voice wound down.

Margaret nodded and picked up her purse. Now perhaps Ken would turn and walk back. But Simon and Dianne were the ones coming down the aisle. Simon was pale, under the sunburn, and his look was not of a dynamo but of a man under strain—she saw Dianne regard him solicitously and steady his elbow as they walked. But there was no forgetting he was a candidate. He shook hands with Ken, and stopped for a quick chat with a couple beside him, and had words for a woman still hunched over on her seat, and then stopped to talk to Margaret. She was a good sport to have come. He really appreciated it. What a week she had had. Then the keen eyes went to the woman beside her. "You too, Alice. To make time on one of your busy days—we really are grateful." At which point a slight touch of Dianne's hand told him it was all right to go.

"Tough for him," the woman called Alice said.

"Very." She stared ahead: Ken was still up there, talking to one of the cousins.

"Why'd he say you had had a week?"

"Oh, I'm Margaret Berringer. I was the one to find Myra. Also, my brother David . . ." Her voice trailed off. Maybe this is how she'll go through life from now on: sister of suspect number one.

Alice buttoned her jacket. "Would you like to go for a cup of coffee? Seems so incomplete this way."

Incomplete: yes. But when Ken finally caught up with them, just after they went out the door, this particular completion offered no comfort. "How are you doing, Alice?" he said to the woman. "You're looking good." To Margaret he said only, "So you're still at it," before he walked away.

She and Alice crossed the street, to a place Alice said she knew on the next block. Margaret suddenly found herself shaking; she needed to sit, to catch her breath, to drink something hot. She was glad Alice didn't talk until the coffee was in front of them. Then she said again that everyone had done very well, considering.

Margaret buttered a muffin and put it down. "Not Ken Ash."

"You mean his snippy greeting to you—it was odd. Not like him. Do you understand why?"

"He thinks I'm trying to pry. Find out who killed Sandy."

"And are you?"

Well, why else did she call Dianne last night, and inquire about funeral plans, and get onto what turned out to be an exclusive list of funeral guests, if not to keep prying? "I guess you could say so. My brother—well, you must read the papers like everyone else. Yes, I would like the police to be more assiduous in finding out who killed Sandy Fleming."

"So you think maybe you'll help them along," Alice said in her calmly decisive voice. "Well, it's true, something like that would be offensive to Ken. He's a man with a very strict sense of classifications; maybe it has to do with being an architect. According to his orderly way of thinking—I'm guessing now, but it seems logical—detective work should be left to detectives."

She guessed right, this woman with the sharp, shrewd, pretty features.

"And seeing us together," Alice went on, "that probably didn't help your cause either."

"Us?"

"Since as his ex-wife I'm a part of his past and you may be trying to zero in on that past. He probably thinks you deliberately chose me to sit next to."

"You were married to Ken!" Alice: of course.

The direct gaze looked her over. "Does it trouble you?"

"Of course not."

"Are you in love with him?"

She remembered what Ken had said. A no-nonsense psychiatrist. Does this give her the right to put this kind of impudent question? "Why in the world should you think that?"

"You seem so concerned with what he thinks."

"We've spent exactly two hours with each other," she said stiffly.

"It can happen in one."

"Besides..."

"Besides, now he's angry at you. My dear, I'll explain to him that our being together was pure accident."

It struck Margaret that she was the one entitled to anger. Why does she have to keep being so defensive, explaining herself, justifying? "Listen. Why shouldn't I try to find out anything? They can't arrest my brother, they haven't any proof, but how long is he supposed to go on like this? Prime suspect in a murder case."

Alice buttered another muffin. "Tell me about your brother."

"There's nothing to tell. He's paralyzed from the waist down. That's his life."

"You mean, he doesn't work?"

She watched a woman with two boys squeeze into the table beside them. "Know what? Be easier if he didn't have all that money. If he were absolutely forced to go someplace from nine to five and do something. Filing cards. Programming a computer. Writing reports. I don't know. Anything to take him out of himself." One of the boys looked up, she must be talking too loud. Too loud, too much—what's got into her! "Or if he had to join some group. If he weren't capable of buying every piece of equipment and getting every kind of treatment for himself. Even if once in a while he'd see others in the same boat. But he never will. Communal. In his book that's the second worst word. The worst is irreversible. Don't mind me, I never carry on like this. It's just, I guess, having been at a funeral."

Alice wiped butter from her lips. "How about anyone to share the load with you? Does he have a wife?"

She looked down at her cup. "His wife left him."

"Ah, well, they often do. They say they won't, those distraught spouses, they make all the protestations about loyalty and affection. But when push comes to shove, they're finished. And no other siblings? No trusted friends? How about you? Do you have a husband?" Alice pushed away her plate: decisive gestures to match her decisive thinking.

"We were divorced a year ago."

"Your brother's accident break that up too?"

"How'd you guess?"

Alice looked sideways.

"He thought I was giving David too much attention. He was right. I did give him too much attention, it drove Alex up a wall. Sometimes I think we'd have broken up anyhow, we were at a stage where things weren't good between us. You might say basically we didn't approve of each other. On the other hand, sometimes when an empty apartment seems intolerable, or the phone doesn't ring, or I sit down to yogurt for supper, well, I think why didn't I put up a fight for him, we could have stumbled on together for a few more years."

"In any case, seems the problem is on you; you have it alone. And incidentally, you'll have to bear it if he turns out to be guilty."

Another one with the message. "Oh, look here—"

"I'm not saying there's proof of that," Alice said calmly. "Or that there ever will be. But suppose in your heart it's what you believe. Your brother killed Sandy. How would it affect you? Would you cut down on your visits to this difficult and doubtless irascible man? Would you give in to the human inclination not to visit at all? Would the reluctance show on your face each time you bent over to kiss him?"

Very different from the forthright assumption by Alex. Different, subtler, harder to evade. "Listen, I—"

"You're the one holding the bag, you just said so," Alice went on in her voice of offhand certitude. "Well, then, if you were convinced of his guilt, would you drop it? Or could you rationalize infirmity as granting some extra dispensation? Could you act as if you cared for him as much as ever? *Would* you still care for him as much as ever? What I suppose it comes down to, would you be able to reconcile yourself to the idea of murder?"

Why don't I stop her, a stranger, as she sits across from me going into these private, these inadmissible matters? She felt Alice looking at her.

"My dear, have I got you upset?"

"A little."

At the next table, an altercation. One boy is happy with the ice cream he has ordered, the other says why'd they have to come here, not even any pizza, why can't they go where there is pizza. As if reminded, Alice looked in her cup, which was empty. "Will you have more coffee? And maybe some pie? The apple pie here is really not bad. Well, mind if I do?" She signaled the waitress. Then she said the picture was not clear-cut. There might be a number of people besides David Bynam with a reason for wanting Sandy dead.

What a woman: she gives with one hand and takes with the other. "What kind of people?"

Alice made room for the apple pie on the table. "You don't conduct a succession of love affairs without making for some bad feeling—Oh, come on. You did know, didn't you?"

"I've sort of been gathering."

"Some men can get away with it. They keep it up for years, no enemies, no one wanting to have their head. Because nobody knows. Their home life in one compartment, their love life in another. But Sandy wouldn't have it that way. The furtive little lunch in some back-street restaurant—not for him, not for him. If he was having an affair, they ate at whatever place was the favorite. They had to go dancing at the most popular night spot. They walked hand in hand through Kennedy on the way to some Caribbean weekend. That was his personality. Expansive. Open. Not that he wanted to hurt Myra, or the abandoned husband, or the previous woman who had just been discarded. Just the opposite. He felt great tenderness toward all of them. Especially Myra. He knew all Myra's problems; last thing he wanted was to add to them. But he was simply no good at practicing concealment. My dear, you should have tried this pie.''

She can't think of food. What she sees is that girl in Chicago. That neat compact figure, the credulous talk. After a while would she also have joined the line of sad or accepting or vengeful discards?

''What makes a man act like that? Interesting question,'' Alice said, as if Margaret was the one to ask it. ''Not just a craving for living well, though of course he had that. But for living well in public. Showiness for its own sake. If you have it, flaunt it. What it comes down to, he couldn't be cramped. Secrecy to him wasn't just a nuisance, it was a deprivation. It actively curtailed his pleasure.''

At the next table, at last a settlement: they will have ice cream here, go to the next block for pizza. Margaret watched the mother sit back with the complacence of the successful mediator. Then she asked whether some of the women didn't have their own reasons for keeping things quiet.

''Well, yes. For some a ban was very important. One, I remember, was a young girl who was engaged, who had no intention of breaking her engagement but couldn't resist a final fling with Sandy. Another was a law student who somehow got the idea that the taint of adultery would blacken her character when she wanted to be admitted to the bar. As for me, I didn't exactly want it publicized either.''

''You!''

The shrewd face looked up. "Does it shock you that I had an affair with Sandy Fleming?"

No. Yes. YES. "I am surprised."

"Neither Myra nor Sandy was in treatment with me," she said with her decisive calm. "There was no problem about unprofessionalism. But still I really did try to keep the lid on. In fact, I made it a requisite. Sex and secrecy, a package deal. On my part I went in for lots of uncomfortable deceit. I had some very inventive stratagems. But you couldn't deter Sandy. An irresistible man and also an irrepressible one. Charm along with a great carelessness. I don't even remember what grandiose gesture it was that gave the game away. A marvelous piece of jewelry he couldn't resist sending? A gorgeous bunch of flowers? A passionate phone call when he might have known I wouldn't be alone? Or maybe it was just that when he and I met at a party, he looked at me with that outspoken ardor shining out of his sweet round eyes." Alice took out a compact and began putting on lipstick. "Whatever it was, Ken got the point," she said through pursed lips.

"It was when you were married to Ken!"

"Why else would we have been divorced? Why would anyone get divorced from a nice guy like Kenneth Ash?"

She knew she should start assembling her things, reaching for the check, but she couldn't move. "You mean, *he* wanted the divorce?"

"I surely didn't." Her head gave a decisive shake. "But that's Ken. If his wife is sleeping with his partner, something has to give. To his mind, there's a derangement. That natural order he cherishes is upset. So he had to remedy it. The remedy was getting rid of the wife." The green pillbox was sitting neatly on her hair, but she adjusted it. "I was really sorry. But I knew there was no use arguing. Along with the niceness—I guess you've noticed—there's a certain inflexibility. Ken, it was clear, would never relent."

"How did he feel about the partner?"

"Another interesting question," Alice said in her didactic way. "Ken didn't discuss his thinking with me, but I think I can state it fairly. With a partner, there's no question of betrayal. Sex is outside the area defined by business relationships. Or to put it another way, who one's partner sleeps with is not a matter to affect those attributes that are important to keeping a partnership on course."

Margaret looked in vain for some clue on that sharp pretty face. "Wasn't Ken even angry at Sandy?"

"Discerning of you to ask," Alice said. "He's no longer angry at me. You saw that. Why should he be, he got rid of his anger in the most positive way, by booting out the instigator of it. And on the surface, he and Sandy always had ideal relations. Two creative men working together, exchanging ideas, assigning credit—utmost harmony. But I've always thought that under it Ken carried around a load of resentment, he must have, the more virulent for having to be repressed."

Why is she telling me this? What does it mean? What does she want me to think it means? Is it just the maunderings let loose, in her as in everyone, by the sentimentality of a funeral? Or did she deliberately embark on this when she heard what I was here to find out?

Alice checked her watch. "This is so interesting. I wish I could stay. But a patient in twenty minutes—No, my dear, put that away. I suggested this, I'm paying."

But a quizzical look on the sharp features, as if she knew perfectly well that so far as the particular patient she had just had coffee with was concerned, the session had introduced more questions than it had solved.

SIXTEEN

SHE SAT AT THE TABLE after Alice left; her inclination was to keep sitting. Stay on in this indifferent, overheated coffee shop and think about the new pictures that have been insinuated. Ken working in the office next to Sandy, Ken studying Sandy's plans for a building's extension, Ken revising the bid he and Sandy worked on last week, all that communal and productive enterprise, when all the time he thinks, he can't help thinking, last night that bastard was in bed with my wife.

You'll find out more than you want to: Erica. Well, Erica honey, right again. I don't want to know it. I wish I could expunge it. If only Ken need never discover that I learned it.

"Will you be having anything else, ma'am?"

"I'm just going." Going to see Helene, who was one of my main reasons for attending the funeral, who by rights should have been there. She looked in her pocketbook for the piece of paper on which she'd written the address after Helene gave it to the policemen. An address but no phone number, which is probably just as well. On the phone, someone can put you off, say this terrible backache, my cousin from out of town, urgent appointment in fifteen minutes, whereas face to face they have no choice except to murmur wanly, well, sure, come on in.

Some people, at any rate, have no choice. Helene lived in one of the brownstones in the East Nineties that have been converted, with some taste and considerable expense, to apartments; interesting, Margaret thought as she pressed the intercom bell, that someone working as a domestic should be able to afford this.

"Helene? It's Margaret Berringer. You remember, we were together when—" Two women in raincoats came out, and her voice dropped. When Myra Fleming was found dead—not something you care to shout into the disheartening receptacle of a public intercom. But Helene's voice after a pause said Oh, and after a longer pause it allowed that she would come right down.

Margaret looked at the sky, which was getting darker. Of course that wary woman would want to come down, look over a visitor before letting her in out of this miserable weather. Even a visitor whose name she surely recognizes, under circumstances she could not possibly forget. But when Helene appeared she had put a brown coat over her dress, and she let the door close behind her as she stood next to Margaret on the street.

"Helene, am I interrupting something? Will you forgive me for coming without notice?" Helene's face registered nothing, so, talking fast, she went on. All that confusion the other day, the two of them really didn't have a chance— anyhow, Margaret hoped they might now go someplace for a few minutes and talk.

Helene pushed the top coat button through a tight buttonhole. The wooden look, Margaret thought, was more noticeable here than in the Fleming kitchen. For someone who works as a maid, the negative appearance is the preferable one. She is there to enhance things not by adorning herself but by polishing the silver; her main duty to the background is to fade into it; when she brings in afternoon tea, it is the tea service, the flowered cups, the small sandwiches that should get the attention. But we're on her own territory now. Her own street. Does she still have to flaunt that inaccessible gaze, as if to hold the interest of a stranger at bay?

"I did want to ask you about Myra Fleming," Margaret went on.

"The police say it's all right."

All right? Then she realized. Helene is in the clear. Those three hours on the town have been checked out. "Well, of course. But you see, it's not all right for my brother. He's a paraplegic—you know, his legs are paralyzed—obviously he couldn't have killed Myra, that studio three flights up. But there's a suspicion he might have killed her husband—Oh, Helene, it's a nightmare. Anyhow, if it turns out that Myra didn't commit suicide at all, in which case whoever killed her could also have been the one to kill her husband . . ."

The dismissive stare again. Everyone starts at the word "paraplegic," puts on at least a routine show of sympathy, but not this woman. All right, keep going.

"I was thinking about Myra. A woman like that. Someone so weak and indecisive. I can't imagine her taking a gun and shooting herself. If she were desperate, okay, she might swallow a bottle of sleeping pills. Or maybe even get into a bathtub and slit her wrists. But to hold a gun against her own breast, an act so physically destructive—Helene, what do you think?"

A mistake. Helene is not going to venture an opinion. Standing with her hair lank on either side, her eyes neutral, her body encased in the stiff column of a coat, the last thing she will do is venture an opinion.

"I mean, did you even know she had a gun? Did you ever see one?"

For answer, Helene looked up: a fine drizzle starting. Now surely she will say, let's go inside. But she moved closer to the wall, where an overhang protected them from the wet.

"She wouldn't have shown it to you, of course. But was there some closet where you were not supposed to go? Did she, for instance, ever get excited when you opened the wrong drawer? Not that it would be conclusive, but did she seem to be hiding something? No? You're sure of that?"

Not a drizzle at all, a steady rain that despite the overhang streamed against them. Maybe she doesn't have a real apartment, just an inadequate space carved out of what was once something grand and spacious. Or she's in some basement quarters, not quite legal, vaguely habitable; they try to utilize every inch in these renovations. That squalid place, she's ashamed, that's why she won't ask me to come in.

"Okay, no proof one way or other about a gun. But, Helene, do you remember that terrible day? When we found her? I mean, think back a minute," she said in her mesmerizing voice. "There you were in the studio with Myra and this visitor. You went downstairs and wrapped a picture for him. You brought it back. The man took it out. Remember all that? Then what happened?"

"She went to the phone."

Margaret stared. Dear Lord, it's working. She's back there, reliving it, letting the sequences take shape. The phone: something of substance she has let slip.

"Who did she call?"

"I don't know."

"But you heard something, you must have. Which phone did she use?"

"In the living room."

"And you were right there in the hall, weren't you? Or even in the kitchen. That big house, with the open spaces—sound travels. What'd she say?"

"I don't know."

"A business call? Something to do with money? Or maybe a friend to tell them about her visitor?"

"She said something about wanting to see them." Another offering—having given it, Helene pulled her shoulders together, as if to withdraw from her own liberality.

"She wanted to see someone. Ah. But she didn't want you around during the visit so she told you to go out. Helene, any clues about who it was? A man? A woman?"

No answer. Margaret studied that dismissive face, and an idea suddenly struck. Sandy seduced her, as obviously he could seduce anyone. She was on hand, a constant presence, a woman of passable looks and appropriate age, and one afternoon when Myra was out he made love to her, and after that he ignored her, and that explains not only her circumspection today but her impassivity when Myra was found dead on her studio floor. Then Margaret pulled up her damp collar. What am I thinking! A woman so wooden, so sexless, as if the warmth of sensuality had been drained out of her—not for Sandy Fleming, never for Sandy Fleming. He liked women who were trim, bright, decisive, open, women with a message of their availability shining out of their lively eyes. Women like Alice and Leni and, doubtless, that wary law student and the girl resolved to keep both her engagement and her fling with Sandy, and . . . well, others. Plenty of others. But not his woman, no, impossible.

"Helene, please try to think. Did it sound like a friend she was talking to? Someone she knew well? Or a stranger? If you knew how important... I've been trying for days. I even went to the funeral, I thought I'd see you."

"Funeral?" Helene looked sideways, where a man walked by under an umbrella.

"For Myra Fleming. I just came from there."

"They said there wouldn't be one." A flicker of spirit at last.

"Who said?"

The wind shifted, rain beat against their faces. "I found a number in her phone book that last day when I was cleaning up," Helene said. "A brother? Someone with the same name anyhow. I called, and they said no funeral."

Margaret frowned. A touch of snobbery, after all? From Dianne, with her soft ringlets, her lilting voice? Or was it Simon, that dynamic candidate, muffing this one encounter because of the cumulative strain the past week had brought? "Just a very small funeral," she said. "Not really a service." She shivered. Water was seeping in through her shoes."

"I can't talk now," Helene suddenly said. "I have to go."

"Are you going someplace? I'll walk with you."

"No," Helene said. "No."

It was the funeral, that auspicious ceremony to which a domestic had been uninvited. She had lost ground by mentioning it, touched some sensitive nerve. "Helene, please can't we go inside for just a minute? Just stand in there out of the rain?"

Helene was moving toward the door. "Come back tomorrow," she said.

"What's that?"

"Tomorrow."

"But I really have to—What time tomorrow?"

Helene had her key in the door. "Eleven o'clock," she said.

"Then we can talk? We can sit down and go through it? All the details? Oh, Helene, I'll surely be here." But the last words were spoken to the street, because the door closed, the brown coat had slipped through it.

When Margaret moved sideways, rain from the overhang cascaded onto her hair and shoulders; it matched the frenzy suddenly streaming within. She wanted to press the bell, lean on it, shout her irate message like some frustrated peddler of magazine subscriptions. Helene, this is crazy, it's not fair, it makes no sense. What small satisfaction does it give you to put me off till tomorrow when I'm right here today? Are you punishing me for what someone else did? I can't help it about the damn funeral; I'm not the one who was too snobby to tell you where it was. Or maybe this is just one of those aimless exercises of power some people get their kicks out of. Well, I'll fix you, I'll stand here ringing this bell till you have no choice, you'll have to come down and get it over.

She saw a man eyeing her—had she been talking out loud? She walked to the corner and hailed a cab. Her suit is a mess; even after a trip to the cleaner's the pleated skirt will never be the same. And there is mud on her suede shoes, and water trickling under her collar may already have stained her silk blouse.

Well, she'd made two mistakes. One was to wear her suede shoes and pleated skirt to the funeral in the mistaken idea that Kenneth Ash, against all logic, would be smitten with her appearance, and the second was in going empty-handed to Helene: a lady bountiful who carried no bounty. A maid, Myra's maid—someone who went every day to clean and wash and brown the stew for another woman's dinner—money might be too crude, but surely a visitor might have brought something. Flowers. Candy. Liquor. Cake. Something at once to disarm the rigidity and acknowledge the indebtedness.

Next morning she settled on cake—small rich honey buns suitable for one who, by all evidence, lived alone. And it was a fine day, a glorious day—with the sun shining she noticed the red painted door, the flower boxes on either side, the brass knocker. She pressed tentatively on the bell, and then harder; even if Helene doesn't care to ask me up, she's still ashamed about that squalid interior, there's nothing to stop us from standing right here and talking.

Another ring. People don't sit around waiting, even when the exact hour has been agreed. They take laundry down to the washing machine in the cellar. They run upstairs to ask a neighbor for some black thread. They doze while watching television. They go around the corner to pick up milk and eggs. But when Margaret looked up the block, no trace of a woman in a cylindrical brown coat, only three girls in shorts, beating the season.

Panic builds slowly, especially against a tide of high hopes. She shifted the cake box. She peered through the glass partition. Absurdly, because Helene's name was listed on a white card, she checked the address in her pocket-book. It wasn't till she went to the corner and looked into the small grocery store and ran back that the frenzy took hold; she was no longer a sedate visitor who had somehow mistaken a time or place; she was someone wildly pressing every button at once.

Though several voices made indignant queries, only one person came down—a woman who was less annoyed than she might have been. She jangled the two dozen keys on a chain around her waist, she poked at the towel wrapped around her hair, she said querulously she wasn't even allowed to wash her hair in peace, but she seemed less annoyed at the intrusion than interested by it. A visitor for Helene Maas? That so, an appointment, even? My heavens. Because Helene never got visitors, so what a pity that when one finally comes it should be after Helene has left.

"She left?"

"Nine this morning. Sorry, miss, you had to come for nothing."

Margaret looked up the stairs, which were clean and well lit and covered by a maroon rug. Then she sat on the bottom one. "I'll wait here. I don't care how long it takes. You don't mind if I wait, do you?"

"Miss!" The woman's voice was sharp, but it had kindly overtones. "What I mean, she cleared out. One two three."

"Cleared out?" She had a sudden vision of Helene with a broom, working the corners, reaching under beds—in the next instant, she knew it wasn't that.

"Nine o'clock," the woman repeated. "Took her two suitcases and good-bye."

Margaret could feel her face burning—does despair come out in red splotches on one's cheeks? "She told me eleven," she said, as a door opened on a floor above, a woman leading a dog came down. "Mrs. Apter, think they'll fix that faucet today?" Under the towel, Mrs. Apter put on a look of regal speculation. Yes, she did think so. Then no more conversation till the front door closed on the dog and misery asserted its claim once more.

"Where'd she go?"

Mrs. Apter didn't know.

"But that's not—I mean, people leave forwarding addresses."

Some people. Mrs. Apter shrugged.

"Or a message. There has to be one someplace."

Mrs. Apter rearranged the towel. "A message? She'd leave it with me. They all do. If they want someone to find them home, if they absolutely don't want it, if the husband isn't supposed to catch on to where the wife is, if the wife is trying to keep tabs on where the husband goes—twenty apartments, you wouldn't believe the stories I carry in my head." She jangled the keys as if to demonstrate their potency: they unlocked apartment doors and also life histories; she was the repository of complaints about the plumbing and confidences about marital conflict.

Someone else coming down. Morning, Mr. Sincox. Morning, Mrs. Apter. Another wait till the coast was clear—then Margaret looked up. "Listen. Could I see where she lived? Oh, it's not that I don't believe, it's just . . . And this cake. I brought it for her. Honey buns. Could you possibly use some honey buns? Yes, please take it."

The cake did it. Or possibly she'd have been granted permission anyhow—Mrs. Apter said she'd been about to go in. You had to get right to work. Even an apartment that the rent's paid till the end of the month. Otherwise they think you're not doing your job—Here we are, Miss.

Margaret stood at the door. Squalor? This pleasant room with two windows, blond wood furniture, a serviceable kitchen at one end—how could Helene afford it? More to the point, how could she have found it? A newcomer, someone not wise to the configurations of a drastic housing shortage, how could she have come from another country and latched on to this furnished room in a presentable apartment house in a nice neighborhood?

"I really came to ask her questions. That's why—"

"You mean about that couple she worked for? Both gone, poor things. Don't be surprised. I told you I know everything. I don't always let on, but I know. It comes with experience. No secrets from the super, that's the way it is." Mrs. Apter heaved a contented sigh. That inclusive view into twenty lives—it was a fringe benefit, possibly the main one, of her job: drudgery balanced by omniscience.

Margaret said that was right: both Mr. and Mrs. Fleming dead. So what she wondered was, first, how did Helene get this apartment?

"He got it for her. Fleming, yes, that's it. Short man with a round face and this sweet smile. At least, I thought it was sweet."

You and how many others.

"He said a woman was coming to work for him as a maid; he wanted her to have a decent place. He'd be the one on the lease and be paying the rent. I don't usually go for that arrangement, but he had the gift of gab, you couldn't turn him down, know what I mean?"

Yes.

"Can't say I had any cause for regrets." Mrs. Apter dislodged the towel; under it was a forest of curlers. "Never any trouble about the money from him, and no fuss or noise from her. Not even any company that I ever saw."

The same suspicion brushed briefly against her. Sandy and Helene? Never. No matter how much inexplicable liberality the job dispensed, how seemingly disproportionate its perquisites, never, never.

Margaret walked around the room. Blankets folded neatly, hangers empty, a rag rug washed and left over a chair to dry. Some of this must have belonged to Helene. Didn't she want it, Margaret asked.

"She said I could keep the lot. Now she'd come into the money, she couldn't be bothered with stuff like that."

"Money? I don't understand."

"At first I didn't either. Couldn't figure what she was getting at when she knocked at my door. Finally she said I had to come see for myself, she half pulled me. My heavens. Can't say I blamed her. Money spilling out of a suit-case like one of those gangster movies.''

''Money? Suitcase?'' Her stilted voice, capable of noth-ing but this mindless echo.

''First I thought it was a fake. Those pictures on the pa-per money like no pictures on money that I ever saw. But she said it was all right. English currency, she said. What they use where she came from.''

''Bermuda,'' Margaret murmured.

Mrs. Apter tested a rolled-up curl. Still wet. ''She counted it while I was here. Sat right where you are now and counted the lot. Equal to ten thousand American dollars, she said. Enough for a down payment on a house down there.''

''House.'' Still the hollow repetitions, as though issuing of their own accord. ''Back to Bermuda, that's where she's going?''

''Sure thing. There was an airplane ticket too, in with the money. For today.''

Margaret suddenly stood up. ''What time is that plane?'' Fury seized her. She will dash to the airport, track Helene down, say you can't leave until you tell me everything. But in a voice tinged with sympathy, Mrs. Apter said an eleven o'clock plane. Helene had been taking no chances. The money came at seven-thirty—by nine she was packed and gone.

No chances: you can say that again. No way she was going to be stopped by the inconvenient questions of an impor-tunate visitor.

''Listen. This windfall—the English money. Where did it come from?''

''Some messenger brought it. Boy in uniform.''

''You mean she didn't know where?''

''Oh, she knew all right.'' Mrs. Apter wound up another curl and clipped the curler back on. ''It was from her lady. The one she worked for. Mrs. Fleming—that's right. There was a note that said the lady left it to her in her will.''

"But—" Margaret stopped. Her jaw felt rigid.

"Seems a pile of money, doesn't it? Even if she was the best maid in the world, my heavens, someone who's worked for you just eight months. Well, she took it in stride, I'll say that. Like she took everything. She said something terrible happened to her long ago, it was time something good did."

"Did she say what the something terrible was?"

"Not her. She was no big talker, that one. Didn't talk, didn't get excited—no way you could get a rise out of her. One day last month we had a break-in. Couple of apartments on floors one and two. So all the tenants are blowing their top, call the police, call the owners, get better locks, everything. All the tenants, but not her. Miss cool and collected through the whole thing. Like she's not even part of the house. It's not natural, know what I mean?"

"Yes."

"Search me what her terrible something was, someone like that, a waste of time to ask questions." The tone might be truculent, but the gaze under the overhanging towel was wistful: for once her privileged position hadn't granted her access to all the facts. Somewhere along the way, a life history had eluded her, refused to release its full fascinating weight.

Margaret studied the room. Not quite cleared out after all. A single slipper at the bottom of the closet, a rolled-up tube of toothpaste and some bottles of pills in the medicine cabinet, boxes of powdered soup in the kitchen. That was nothing, Mrs. Apter said. Margaret should see the mess some of them left. You picked up for days, and then you still had to get in the handyman and painters. She figured a day's work here and she'd have it in shape. That Helene, as tenants went, no complaints.

No complaints from Helene either. It's money, isn't it? Back home, when she's putting the down payment on a house, no one will ask did it come with the proper credentials, was it presented under the approved auspices? It's only me, the detective manqué, left high and dry at the end of the line, who wants to fill the room with the wail of her fruit-less complaining.

SEVENTEEN

IT WAS FIVE-THIRTY when she got to David's. Her routine hour, which is appropriate: everything will go back to being routine from now on. Because surely that's what characterizes failure—after the grandiose dreams and noble expectations, the knowledge that nothing is going to change, things will plod along in the same course as they did before. She really did expect to make some brilliant discovery. Margaret Berringer was going to find out what a whole police force couldn't. If she talked to enough people and pushed through enough doors, the crucial information would somehow be yielded up. But she's done it. Had all the inquisitive conversations, brought her insight to bear on all the characters, looked into every available corner. And it's finished. There is no one left to talk to, no place left to go. Mission ended; results nil.

She stiffened as usual when she went in, that involuntary gathering of her resources. Garrulity, invention, compassion, tact, or all of these or none of them—who knows what David's bruised sensibility on any day will require. But it was not David who greeted her.

"Thank goodness you're here." A portly figure in his white coat, Lawrence materialized beside the door, as if he had been standing in wait. She looked toward the window, where David always sat in his wheelchair, where he conspicuously was not sitting.

"Anything wrong?"

Lawrence's voice settled into a strained whisper. Not exactly wrong. She should not get excited. Mr. Bynam isn't sick. But he is being difficult.

"Difficult?" She's whispering too. The prevailing characteristic of a house of invalidism: two always in conspiratorial confab against a third. A few days ago she and David had trusted to a closed door to shield their wary talk from Lawrence; often on her visits she sees David and Lawrence exchange the tacit glances that constitute a judgment on her excessive concern or mistaken fears; now she and Lawrence are standing side by side, counting on the expanse of living room and hall to keep their words from David.

The expedient whisper went on. Mr. Bynam, it seems, is in bed. Has been there all day. Won't get up. Not to be fitted into his braces and stand for half an hour, although he knows how important, not even to get washed and changed. And he won't eat, which is bad enough, but he also won't drink, which is infinitely worse; the same glass of water has been next to him for three hours. As for pills, though Mr. Bynam made a show of accepting them, he, Lawrence, spotted two of them on the floor behind the bed; he has a suspicion that if he really looked he would find the others relegated to the same place.

"Why didn't you call me?"

"I did. I've been trying. No answer."

No answer because I was cosseting myself after my futile mission. Stunned with the sense of failure, I tried walking and shopping. I even made a pass at a movie to get myself into the convivial state of mind that's a requisite for a visit here.

"How long has this been going on?"

"All day. That is, since ten when they brought him back."

"They?"

"The police took him out early. They wanted to drive him someplace, I'm just not sure."

She looked at Lawrence's bland face; he probably is sure but considers it just as well not to say.

"Moment he came back he changed into pajamas and got into bed and that was that."

When the whisper ceased, she had the sense of David in his own room, alert, attentive. *He knows I'm here. He's too proud to call out, but of course he knows. He has the preternaturally keen ear of the invalid or the hurt child.*

"Lawrence, I'd better go in." *Into the room that never fails to deliver its shock. In the living room David is a good-looking man who happens to be sitting in a wheelchair. In his own bedroom he wears the graceless malcontent of the invalid. Partly this is the result of a prone position: anyone lying down is invariably more patient than personality; a head on a pillow is a head haloed by infirmity, weakness, pain. But also it is because the paraphernalia to compensate for disability is all around: the odious braces, the movable trolley to accommodate food and drink, the overhead pulleys culminating in a metal grip so the patient can turn himself over, even lift himself from wheelchair to bed, and of course the bed itself, that steely contraption that can be tipped, tilted, lifted, turned, depending on how one's fingers manipulate the panel at one end.*

"Maggie, don't look so grim." *Stealing her thunder. Oh, he's a smart one, her brother.*

"Hi, David."

"Lawrence been filling you in, the old windbag?"

She pulled a chair over to the bed. *Won't even get washed: with that usually meticulous routine gone by the boards, how quickly the faint emanation of invalidism takes hold.* "David, what goes on?"

"Maggie, I had it from him all day. Don't I want to get dressed, how about this nice drink of cranberry juice, now just these two little pills, let's try it in a different glass. Don't you start."

She looked at him, past him; hearing that aggrieved tone, she was back with the early days after the accident. At the start of recovery, there had been a period of euphoria when he felt sure, he knew for certain, his functions would come back. *Impossible they should not.* "What you're feeling is spastic reflexes," the doctor mildly cautioned, but David knew better. That deep-seated will to move he felt within himself must surely translate into an ability to move. When, after all, had the impulses of that awesome will ever failed him before? Which made the reaction when it came that much blacker. "There is no curative treatment for damage to the spinal column," he read to her one day, the tone of one reciting a sacred litany. "Maggie, do you believe me? Says so right here." "David, where'd you get that book?" Out of the hospital library, of course; he'd prevailed on one of the social workers to bring it to him. "So why did they try to kid me before?" She sat silent; no use pointing out to him that he'd been kidding himself. "Extreme maladjustment," was the pained verdict that same social worker passed on to Margaret later on. Barred from David's room, she fluttered miserably before the door in her blue uniform. If the patient would only join the occupational therapy classes, participate in the communal psychotherapy, come to a workshop—make her day! But there he lay, furious, silent, his obdurate despair a measure of her stunned ineptitude.

The same inept expression, doubtless, on her own face now, Margaret thought. And the same pattern from David. It was what she had been afraid of. That euphoria when he found himself relishing the dazzlement of being in the public eye—and then the reaction. The public eye, it turns out, is cold and hostile. No one will bring about a miracle. There is no curative treatment for murder. She looked over at the braces, which Lawrence had not put back in their special closet but left as if for an object lesson against the wall. That contraption of leather and metal and hooks and hinges.

"Interesting, aren't they?" David said. "Like some obscene surrealist sculpture. What would you call it? Standing Exhibit? Standing Tall? Or maybe just Still Life—Very Still."

"David, cut it out."

"Oh, they're useful, I admit. Best way for someone in my circumstances to get the normal gravitational stimuli working." The same dry tone in which he had read to her from the medical textbook. "This just happens to be one of the days when I can't work up an interest in the normal gravitational stimuli. I'm tired of placating them."

She lifted her hand and then dropped it. "At least drink some water."

"Did you ever have to down eighteen glasses of liquid a day?"

"Okay, David, okay, you don't have to—"

"Tired of giving all that attention to my urinary tract also." He patted the blanket, as if to dismiss what lay under it.

"You'll have to give a lot more attention if you get an infection."

"I won't let it get to that point."

All right, he's taunting her with something that can be interpreted either way. She won't answer, won't ask for clarification. But after a minute he provided it himself.

"Did you ever think that fifty years ago I wouldn't even be alive? Less than twenty percent of the victims with my kind of fracture survived the first year. For that other eighty percent, perfect solution. Opportune end to all their problems."

And today ninety-five percent survive. Why tell him? He knows as well as she does. She was overcome with a sense of her own helplessness. She and that fluttering social worker and the neurologist and the neurosurgeon and the internist and the rehabilitation engineer and the psychotherapist and the occupational therapist—that whole team up against the canny intelligence and stubborn defiance of one who during those wretched weeks in the hospital amassed all his powers for a policy of noncooperation.

"I've been thinking of how best I could serve the world. People are always telling me I ought to perform some service, I'm in a unique position to do so. Well, you know how I could do it? Do you, Maggie? In a postmortem," he said in his gloating voice, so even through her horror she found herself thinking, Inherent in it is what he wants, to be in control, not subject to doctors' problematic orders or to Lawrence's bought obsequiousness or even to my dutiful affection, but his own man, as he always used to be, the one who runs things.

"Would take some very precise exploration, the incisions done painstakingly from front and back, but they'd make valuable discoveries. Healthy white male in mid-forties, a comparison of the degeneration in vertebrae below the wedge fracture with those—Where are you going?"

"To have you committed," she said. "Let a doctor commit you. If you're going to make these threats, make them to the experts. People who are trained to handle them. Not to someone who loves you. Finds you valuable as you are."

"Maggie, sit down. Here, take this handkerchief. Maggie, I'm sorry."

She said nothing. She felt him take her hand. David wiped perspiration off his face, but he said nothing either; the two of them stayed silent, if not exactly peaceable—only the sound of pots banging in the kitchen told them, was doubtless intended to tell them, that Lawrence was waiting. He had been rendered inert, that gratuitous clanging said: relegated to inaction. The bed, the bath, the braces, the liquids, the massage, the medication—these formed a composite that constituted his patient. Dismantle this composite, upset it, and he had no function. But he'd be ready to start up again, Margaret knew. She just has to say a word—crisis over, or some euphemistic expression thereof—and he would be in here, sleeves rolled up, expression at once censorious and forgiving.

But the crisis isn't over. That David who is more than just bed and bath and braces is no longer making threats, but he hasn't conceded anything either. He's holding himself in

abeyance, waiting. Waiting for what? How am I supposed
to act? What strategy is at my disposal?

"David, what went on with the police?"

"Ha. So Lawrence was talking."

"Is it a secret?"

"No, indeed. I tried to call you. For reasons of his own,
I imagine Lawrence was also trying to call you; all day your
phone's been ringing like mad."

He looked at her, that silent interrogation, but there was
no way she could confide in him the saga of her failed mission, and she asked him again about the police.

"Oh, them. They called last night and said they'd be here
first thing this morning. Really first thing, Lawrence had to
hustle to get me ready. What did they want? A ride back
along the route to the house, that's what. They hoped I
could recognize the body of water in which I threw the gun.
Then they would send divers down after it and they would
have proof. One way or other," he said in the cryptic tone
that never failed to rouse her, press the inevitable questions.

"Could you recognize it?"

"Not a chance. Even though those detectives did their
best. Was it this one? That one? Let's drive over it again,
Mr. Bynam. Hopeless. They all look alike, those bays or
inlets. Especially from a car. Same kid with a bicycle on all
of them, same derelict in a rowboat dangling his ineffectual
fishing rod, same picturesque sprinkling of weeds along the
edge."

"Couldn't you even rule out any?"

"I did say a couple definitely weren't right. Too big, or
the bridge was too high, or the guardrail was unfamiliar, or
the whole terrain didn't ring a bell. And even then it was no
good. We drove over one, I said absolutely not this, and the
detective sitting next to me wrote something in his notebook, and then I looked again, I said, Well, let's see now,

not really positive." With a sudden spasm, he folded the sheet down over the blanket.

"What'd they say?"

"They asked a lot of stupid questions. What kind of throwing ability did I have before the accident? How drastically had my throwing ability been impaired? Did people in my circumstances feel more comfortable knowing they had a gun? Was I of the opinion that all paraplegics should be supplied with guns?"

She knows how he hates it, being categorized not as David Bynam but as a case study: specimen of paralyzed man. "Oh, David, then what?"

"They looked at me as if I was some kind of nut. Not being able to remember something so important."

She moved her chair back so she could see him better: the pasty cheeks, the tight mouth, the miasma of invalidism. As a rule, he went to great lengths not to be seen in bed. Even if he suffered from a fever, a flu, he would insist on being dressed and wheeled inside. Tell them to wait, his stern voice would order. No, only a few minutes more.

"So that's why you come home and get into bed and refuse to do what's vital for your health? Because of the dimwit questions of a couple of dumb detectives?"

His hands continued their unaccustomed plucking at the sheet. "They're not getting anyplace with their investigation."

"I guess not."

More clanging from the kitchen: Lawrence's simpleminded attestation of impatience. Then David lifted his head from the pillow. "Maggie, why don't you take it over?"

"What are you—"

"Dumb detectives—how right you are. All those notebooks, but what do they have in them? Tire marks. Mileages. Heights of bridges. But do they get into the important stuff?"

She spoke through thick lips. What did he think was the important stuff?

"Digging in. Finding out about people. Checking out relationships. Sandy and his partner, for instance. Was everything peachy clean between them? Or did resentments clutter up that tidy office? I know a little about business partners"—the muffled voice he always used when referring to his life before the accident—"for p.r. reasons, they put on a good front, best of pals and all that, but under this useful accommodation there can be real feuding— Maggie, do you follow me?"

"Yes."

"Why do you look so stunned?"

"I just . . . nothing."

"Or the brother. I forget his name, but Sandy talked about him from time to time. Said they were the best of friends, but also said, Why the hell didn't architects make as much as lawyers, seemed to me there was a real grievance gnawing away. Well, maybe that quiet envy symbolized something stronger, deeper."

"Sandy's partner and brother—they probably both have airtight alibis," she said lightly.

He raised himself on one elbow: first sign of animation. "Actually, they don't. The wife didn't either. It's one of the few things a detective let slip. Everyone in this case was having a solitary lunch—his exact words—in an obscure restaurant at the time Sandy was being killed."

"David, listen—"

"I know what you're going to say. Detective work—not for you. Not gentlemanly. Excuse me, ladylike. You need special talents. Well, you have the talents. Talent and insight both—more than those fatheads who ask me about by throwing ability. Questioning people, softening them up so you can question them—it's what you do all day. Weighing facts, figuring out the real meaning behind the glib answer."

She looked up. He had hoisted himself up on the pillow, color in those pallid cheeks at last. Color and some liveliness in his eyes. "Even that Sandy, no angel now I think about it."

"Wasn't he?"

David reached out with an absent air. His hand hovered over the glass of water, closed on it, stayed immobile, brought it to his lips. "First of eighteen, down the hatch!" he said. Then in his new interested voice, he went on. "A couple of times when we were working he went off to make phone calls. Scrupulously private calls that I couldn't hear. Then he'd come back with that look on his face. The faintly salacious glow of a man who has just arranged himself a date for the night—know what I mean?"

"Yes."

"So a man like that, used to indulging himself, who knows what vindictive feelings..." With that same absent air—I'm not really doing this—he took another sip. "And of course that great carelessness—I don't mean just the business with me. Though that might in a way typify it. Maggie, you look doubtful."

She said nothing.

"I'd pay your expenses, of course. Whatever time you lose from the office. Or if you have to go out of town."

"Why should I have to go out of town?"

"Who knows?" David said. "Where did Sandy live when he was young? What was his family like? What kind of adolescence? Anyhow, something from his past, some unfinished business—it can happen like that."

"Can it?"

"Maggie, you're in charge. You're the one to decide what avenues you want to poke around in or which characters are worth checking up on. You with your insight, you're a natural."

She stood at the foot of the bed. "David, what goes on all of a sudden? Those detectives have been at this for days, you seemed to be—"

"Resigned? Well, at the beginning, being suspect number one—it had, I admit, a titillating aspect. But gradually the fun went out, it turned serious."

Again that niggling thought. Did the fun go out because they found out something about him he didn't want them to find? Oh, that's nonsense, of course they didn't.

David put down the glass. "Something about the nasty aspersions on that detective's face when I couldn't remember where I threw the gun. Maggie, what do you say?"

Drumming in her ear are the things she can't say. David, I've done it all. Poked around in all those avenues. Checked out all the characters. Even zeroed in on that flamboyant adolescence. And there's no place left to look. Believe me, Davey, I've shot my bolt.

He swung briefly on the metal grip; man doing what he's supposed to, which is to strengthen the usable muscles. "I know what you're thinking. You won't know what leads to follow. You'll feel stymied. Isn't that right?"

"Yes."

"Just wait. I know you—it'll open up as you go along. One thing leading to another."

"I see."

"Maggie, decide quick. Lawrence is going to split a gut if we don't let him in here pretty soon."

Oh, David, unfair, unfair. So I'm the one keeping you from your vital routines. Me, who a few minutes ago was a captive audience for talk about postmortems.

"Christ, this water tastes awful. Tell Lawrence some fresh juice with ice in it—Maggie, love, you'll do it, won't you?" But his gaze went meaningfully around the room, as if in salute to that unstated, that unstatable quid pro quo: she embarks on an investigation, and he accepts the onerous disciplines needed to keep his body in working order, indeed, to ensure his continued inclusion in that favored ninety-five percent who, despite their impairments, their maladjustments, their bleak moods, nonetheless survive. Blackmail. Blackmail based on affection... the most invidious kind. She went into the kitchen to give Lawrence the update: for the time being at least, crisis over.

EIGHTEEN

FOR THE TIME BEING: the phrase held no comfort by next morning. Because how long can she get away with it, the pretense to David that she's following leads, inventing tactics, digging up crafty and definitive revelations? And how fast, discovering that she is not following leads or inventing tactics, will he revert to depression?

Other questions. How serious is this depression? Is it a trial run or, like the time six months ago when the pile of sleeping pills was found stacked up in his night table, the real thing? "Just remember that it's harmful to argue with him," the doctor she'd gone to for advice had told her then. "Better to express in some sympathetic way that you understand his feeling that life may not seem worth living." Well, but what if the depression this time is of a different nature? What if its source is not that defeated frustration the doctors reasonably take for granted, but something else entirely? And how come her playing detective is able to cure it? Does he really expect her to come up with some answer that will avert from him the official gaze? Or—awful thought but she can't dismiss it—does he simply want her committed to working at this answer, which commitment will dazzle her, which dazzlement will seduce her into mentally absolving him?

Well, when things hit bottom, even the ring of a telephone can be a help. "Mom. Hi."

"Oh, good morning, Erica."

"You sound so—I mean, anything wrong?"

"Why should it be?"

"Anything special about David?"

What good would it do to tell her? How can she possibly tell her? "No more than usual."

"Mom, would you tell me if—I mean, sure you're okay?"

"Erica, I'm fine."

A long pause. In her mind's eye she sees the girl frown into the phone, look thoughtfully out the window, then that speculative frown again. "Well, look, do you have any extra time? Today? Tomorrow? Oh, today would be even better. I need you."

Erica needs her. Heaven. The one remedy to restore her. And the girl knows it. Or, rather, as soon as she heard that deadbeat voice at the other end she sensed what was needed; she didn't have to ask a lot of dumb questions or elicit a lot of painful facts, no, she simply cut through with the prize offering at her disposal. I need you.

Yes, she told Erica, she was still on leave from her office. No, there was nothing for David to occupy her today. Why, yes, she could come to the Center this morning. With her tape recorder? Well, sure. Be there, honey, in half an hour.

It was twenty-five minutes, plus a five-minute hassle to get past the woman in front. Mrs. Berringer? Wait, please. No, she does not have instructions. Another minute until it turned out that the instructions were given to someone who just went off duty, and by then Erica was out front, with her serene smile and official voice making everything right.

"In here, Mom." In here, past the table with pamphlets, and the shelf with T-shirts—MY BODY IS MY OWN—and the glass-covered bookcase, and the orange couch where two women were sitting stiffly. Margaret lowered her eyes. Not fair to add to their distress by staring. But Erica waved cheerfully, so maybe they were not here to report the harrowing thing that had happened last night; they were simply meeting someone or applying for a job or picking up pamphlets or doing research in order to establish a center in their own city.

"What I need you for isn't anything easy," Erica said at once. "I mean, if I could do it myself." She sat on the edge of her desk. "Thing is, one of the trustees is making trouble again. Wondering out loud whether with all the shortage of space and money a center for the treatment of rape victims is really a priority. Mom, don't look so upset. You have to expect it. Like you always told me about housecleaning. You just finish the house, top to bottom, and you have to start all over. Endless. Well, so we think we have the board all sewed up, everyone in favor, and then Trustee X talks to his wife's nephew who's an expert on hospital administration, and he says why do we need a rape clinic?"

Margaret nodded, wholly agreeable to being instructed in tolerance and equanimity by her daughter.

"So what I thought, I'd give him a report on three, no, we decided four sort of typical clients, and he'd see how marvelous, useful, indispensable...well, you get it. Only I can't write worth a hoot, I really—"

"Erica, that's not true, I remember—"

"I know. That theme I wrote in my junior year about women's suffrage. Mom, I know you can't bear to believe anything unfavorable about me, but the truth is I really cannot write. I can organize a dozen prima donnas into a working committee, and I can swing that committee around to my way of thinking, I can even coax an uptight foundation director to open his checkbook, but put me in an empty room with a typewriter..."

Margaret said no one liked to be in an empty room with a typewriter. Then she stood up. "Erica, when must you have it by?"

"Mom, you're an angel." Erica slid down from the desk. She smoothed her skirt, which was tight and purple. "Listen, I'm sorry I said all those things about your solving a murder."

"Don't be sorry. You were right. As a detective, I was a washout. I closed the book on that one." She waited while

Erica picked up the phone and said, Tell them I'll call back. "So how do we get on with this assignment? Conciliating Trustee X?"

"Well, Bess—she's one of our therapists, I guess you never met her—she and I picked out four representative case histories."

"You mean like the movies in which a black, a redneck, a poet, and a plumber are shipwrecked on a desert isle?"

"Shipwrecked is right. Only these women are shipwrecked right here in New York high rises. Mom, would you like coffee? Or tea—I can boil the water on this dandy gadget? Well, then, let's go in to Bess, she expects us."

Bess was an earnest young woman with brown hair pulled straight back over a strong forehead, and the effect of sobriety negated by brown eyes that gazed warmly out of horn-rimmed glasses. And she started right in. Did Mrs. Berringer want to sit at that table? Or would this chair be more comfortable? And her tape machine, right here? Well, then, she'd go at it, and if her voice got indistinct, the way it sometimes did when she was excited, Mrs. Berringer must stop her.

Bess adjusted her glasses so she could look down and also up. "Okay, then, case number one, we'll call her Amy. Amy is twenty-seven, a very articulate young woman who works as an office manager in a company that sells foam rubber. She and her boyfriend shared a ground-floor apartment in a brownstone, only he went away one weekend in August. She left the back door open so her cat could get in and out, and that's when it happened. She picked the rapist out of a lineup, and though the first trial ended in a hung jury, he was convicted in the second trial. But by that time there had been five court appearances—Mrs. Berringer, am I going too fast? Sometimes I swallow my words. Yes, well, Erica said you'd be able to, she said you were a whiz at getting everything important.

"Amy is still working; she kept her job but not her boy-friend, even though they'd been planning to get married in six months. They'd even started to look for a co-op, they thought some place in Queens where the prices made more sense. But the strain of the whole thing—well, maybe I should read you something she wrote a couple of months ago.

"'I was okay till after the first trial, but that finished me. Imagine, a hung jury, even though there was all that evi-dence to point to him. And then having to go through it again, five times, actually, in that awful courtroom. I kept crying. Why did I have to testify again, why did the defense attorney keep asking me all those questions, by then every-one knew perfectly well what had happened. And that courtroom, so many men there. Even those old men who sit around all day, they think it's the best show on earth, a male face everywhere you look.

"'Well, they got him at the second trial, and I thought, okay, now things will be normal again. But they aren't. Maybe they never will be, that's what I think in my worst moments. And I'm still crying. Sometimes I think about suicide, I even plan out the method, but then I think, how dumb, honestly, that's the dumbest thing you can do, kill yourself. And then I think, well, I'm stronger now. I have to be, I lived through it, that proves something, doesn't it?

"'I don't know. Things can go bad on you. Last month I broke up with my boyfriend. It's not his fault, I guess. He came home two hours after it happened; I know he was trying to be helpful, but he said all the wrong things. He blamed me for having left the door open. He said didn't I know what New York was like. And he wanted to take over. He tried to hold me right away, take me to the hospital, get me someone to talk to—him making all the decisions. This sounds crazy, but it was like being raped again. And I was awful to him, I know that, I said if he hadn't gone away for the weekend.

"'I date other men now, but it's not too good. I'm sarcastic lots of the time. And last week I insulted my sister's boyfriend. I didn't mean to, but I did.

"'And I keep wanting to talk about it. I don't know what I'd do if I couldn't talk to someone at the Center. My friends say, Sure, talk to them, but they get embarrassed. They say, Oh yeah, and change the subject. And I never told my parents. They'd just say, Don't live there, come back, why do you live in a place like that? Well, maybe they're right, maybe they are.'

"It ends there," Bess said. "No, there's a little more about her work but I don't suppose you need that. Is that chair comfortable? Should I close the window? Did I talk too fast? Oh, Mrs. Berringer, you're wonderful. Just like Erica said.

"Well, case number two, I call her Mrs. D. She's not the victim, her daughter is. Thirteen years old. The girl was coming home from a movie and he grabbed her and pulled her into an alley. We sent the girl—her name is Margie, let's say—to a child guidance clinic, there's no one here that's right, but the mother's been coming. What I'll read you isn't anything she exactly wrote, it's just the answers to a lot of questions, but I thought you wouldn't want the questions. Am I right? Oh, and there was no trial. It was all set up, but when the girl saw the long desk and the judge and all the people, she got hysterical, and the mother said she wouldn't force her. So anyhow, stop me as usual if I go too fast or there's something you don't understand.

"'No, I haven't been talking about it to Margie. Yes, I know you said I should but what I wish is she would forget it. Talking would just keep it alive, wouldn't it? Besides, if I talk I begin to cry and that can't do her any good.

"'Anyhow, she's hard to talk to. Even before this happened she was sort of the secretive kind. We'd ask her how was the party or did she like the movie, and she'd say, Oh, nothing, or I don't know, or It was okay. Sometimes I wonder, is it because of what happened or would she be like this anyhow? Girls of thirteen—aren't they difficult anyhow? No, I don't mean that, they couldn't be like her. Oh, she whines a lot, she wants lots of attention, she's frightened about going out. And school—that's a real mess. She says the kids tease her and call her names. What names? Oh, asshole, bitch, prostitute, Suzie slut. You wouldn't think thirteen-year-old kids, but that's the way it is. I tell her don't pay attention. Oh, yes, I did that too, talked to her teacher and also the principal, but I guess there's nothing much they can do. Lots of mornings there's just no way I can get her out of the house. She wakes up and says she has a cold or a headache. I know she doesn't but what can you say when she's so unhappy?

"'Yes, sure I try to. I make all her favorite foods, but half the time she leaves it on her plate. All she wants is to eat candy. So then am I supposed to get angry or stop her—I just can't figure it. I want to do things right, but how can you scold her or discipline her after what happened? Oh, it's enough to drive you crazy. And lately she has these nightmares. She wakes up screaming, she says there are all these mice around her bed.

"'Well, sure her father wants to help, but men are funny. He's sorry for her, all right, but he also says, Why didn't she run away or scream? And he didn't want me to take her to a doctor after it happened, he kept making objections—I guess he figured if a doctor didn't say yes, he could pretend nothing really happened. Besides, now he's sick, his ulcers kicking up again, and she thinks it's her fault. She's to blame because her father had to go to the hospital.

"'Yes, I try to, but nothing's really good anymore. Even when I'm with the two younger boys, I don't know how to act. If I'm too nice to them, am I being mean to her? Oh, that doesn't make sense, does it? And I'm always thinking of her, where is she, what's going on with her? Or I think, why'd I let her go to that movie, thirteen years old, why didn't I insist she had to stay home?''"

Bess put down the paper. "I know how you feel. Hard to take. Well, things are somewhat better now. The nightmares are still going on, but they got the girl into a different school where no one knows, that was a couple of months ago. And the father's come once or twice too, that might help things along. Mrs. Berringer, we could stop now, give you a—You sure? You're really not tired? And it's not all confused? Oh, you're terrific. It's what Erica said. She said don't worry how shapeless and mixed up it all seems, leave it to my mother, she'll clear out the deadwood and tidy up the ground so when she's finished all the connections show through.

"Anyhow, the next two cases are shorter. The third, I'll call her Claire, she didn't come to us till six or seven years after it happened. I'm not even sure why she came then. Did she read something? Did someone drag her? Did it get through her head that in a situation like hers there are people who can help? All I know is, she turned up here one day.

"And actually, I don't think we've helped her much. You don't have to make a point of this, obviously, in your report, but I really don't. Too much time had gone by. She had buried it too deep. Buried her emotions about it and in the process all her other emotions too. She was eighteen when it happened. I don't know anything about the man. Just someone in the small town she came from. Someplace where everyone knows how much money you owe the bank and what the story is about your husband's drinking and also the particulars of a young girl being raped. In a place like that, it diminishes her. No matter what anyone says about this being a modern age, it really does diminish her. First she's a valuable piece of sexual property, and then her value has gone way down. She's been defiled. Oh, I know this isn't some backward country, but still in a sense it's true. Worse, in her own eyes she's been defiled.

"I don't suppose there was anyone in that small town she could talk to, and by the time she got to us, not much anyone could do. Oh, she manages all right. She's a typist in the complaint department of one of the big department stores, maybe not the job she thought of back when she had dreams about her future, but she gets by. She has a decent room. She buys clothes. Once in a great while she goes to the movies or a restaurant with one of the girls from the store. If you look at her, you don't see anything to make you suppose she was once a cute sexy little thing, but there are no marks of a tragic outlook either.

"No marks of anything. That's what's so sobering. No emotions, is what it comes down to. It sometimes happens like that. They want to deny their feelings about the rape, so they deny all the other feelings too. Nothing moves this young woman. Nothing gets her excited. No one can get a rise out of her. She came in one day and said her brother was dead. Her only sibling, I know she'd been close to him, killed riding his motorcycle. She did all the right things. Went home for the funeral. Spent three days with her mother. I said, Tell me about it, and it was like she was talking about a movie, a lecture. That deadpan voice. And her face—no affect, no expression. Well, that's what it did to her. Someone who goes through life negating it."

Bess sighed. "Now I'm the one who needs coffee. Hope you don't mind waiting while I—Oh, good. Some of these doughnuts too? I guess I get a little carried away, but I could see her sitting there, that cold fishy look. Damaged property, and she doesn't forget it.

"Anyhow, number four, she's damaged too, but she's fighting against it. A black woman, and she knew the man. Or at least she knew who he was. Someone who lived in her housing project. She'd seen him once or twice, playing with his children. That's right, a family man. And she didn't report him. She said—wait a second, we have a statement from her too.

"'I wanted to turn him in, but I didn't. A man, a black man, with a wife, three kids, his mother living with him—I'd ruin him. Hurt his whole family. How could I do it? Only what I didn't realize was how hurt I was going to be. My husband says, Calm down, not so terrible, but he doesn't understand how vulnerable you can feel afterwards. I'm angry at being so vulnerable. Angry at being a woman things like this can happen to.

"'First I tried to act like it never happened. When my next birthday came around, I said I was a year younger than I was. Isn't that crazy? I figured to erase a whole year, the year it happened in. I did that every year for three years. Then I went to this therapist, he asked me did I enjoy it? That's the honest to god truth, what that man said, did I enjoy it? Know what he should have asked? Can I enjoy sex anymore with my own husband? I can admit it here—the answer is no. It's not his fault. Christ, no. He just gets in some position, or uses some gesture, and it reminds me.

"'I'm sick lots of the time. Headache, cold, nausea, flu, you name it. Me, that never was sick in my life. And I'm way too fat, I know it, look at how this zipper doesn't even close. But I sit down at the table, I just feel I want to stuff myself. And I'm scared. Even when someone yells on the street. Hiya, babe, something like that, a bunch of men standing around, I know they don't mean anything—well, still I get all clammy. I think, What do they want? Will they follow me? The subway, that's the worst of all. I can't take it. My husband says, What goes on, all that money for taxis, but I go down the subway, all those people crowded together, all I can think of is which of them is fixing to harm me.

"'Well, maybe someday it'll get better. Last birthday, I said thirty-four. That's my real age. Maybe I'm getting over it, maybe I am.'"

Bess put down her notebook. "That's about it. The four of them. Anything you want to ask? Any extra details? I think you're great to do this. To be able to, I mean. Give me a report like this to write, something, you know, that's important for persuading someone, and I make all kinds of excuses. I have a headache. I need to water my plants. My back hurts. I should look for a present for my mother's birthday. But you, you can take this mess and make something coherent? Like Erica says, clean out the deadwood? Well, a complicated story, I'll be interested to see how it all comes out.''

"Me too," Margaret said. "I'll be very interested to see how it comes out."

NINETEEN

"I WANT YOU to do me a big favor," Margaret said.

From the other end of the phone, which Ken Ash was holding, unencouraging silence.

"It won't take long," she said. "Only a couple of hours."

"A couple of hours when?"

"Tonight," she said, and coughed. "Six o'clock."

"Afraid that's impossible," he said. "There's an opening I have to go to, a painter I've known for fifteen—"

"Tell your painter friend you'll see his pictures tomorrow."

Another silence. Then, "You haven't mentioned what's so important that I should insult a friend of fifteen years' standing."

"Oh, well, I want you to drive with me to Simon Fleming's. He expects us," she added.

"I don't know why he should expect me when—"

"Not the whole evening. Just a half-hour visit," she said.

"Could I know the point to this half hour?"

Her glance went sideways, where the papers she was working on for Erica were spread. Each section was turning out longer than she had expected. "Well, yes. I want to clear out the underbrush and tidy up the ground so when I'm finished the connections show through."

"What'd you say?"

"I'll pick you up at your office at six. I rented a car."

"Look here. Are you planning one of those—what do they call them?—confrontations? Everyone gets together and goes in for chatty remarks, and undermined by all the casualness the villain says Yes, I did it?"

"No confrontation. Ken, please. Just come."

He was waiting in front of the building when she drove up. He even said he'd drive, yes, he'd like to, and in the confusion attendant on her sliding over and dropping her pocketbook and fumbling for it under the seat and waving off the honking car behind and honking in turn to the car in front that sensed there would be a parking space and was not going to budge till that critical matter was resolved, in that disorder, she thought a kind of friendliness had been established. She was wrong. He said yes, he knew the way, he and Sandy had been up here a couple of times when Simon and his wife were thinking of doing some renovations, but that was all he said. After that, purposeful silence.

Well, the silence of two people side by side in the front seat of a car—it can have a convivial aspect. The relaxed stillness of people who know they are thinking the same thoughts, abstaining from the same effort, experiencing a joint fatigue. Or even strangers, if they barely know each other, if they feel the essence of courtesy is to refrain from the kind of automatic talk that can only mean nosy questions, reluctant answers. She and Ken have already experienced the latter; hanging over them is the memory of that lunch: intimacy, sharing, sympathy, laughs. She reached to turn on the radio and then dropped her hand: if he doesn't suggest something to break this unnatural hush, she's damned if she will.

Besides, maybe this is the way he wants it: undisguised ill will. And he's certainly under some great strain. Because this can't be the way he usually drives: the jolting stops after wayward accelerations, the horn-blowing at some car in front that doesn't immediately start up when the light changes, the maneuvering to get into the lane on the left, and then, with a vicious wrench of the wheel, the switch back to the right. A man beside himself.

And he did break the silence once. "Enjoy your talk with Alice?"

She started. She tried to think of some telling retort.

"Don't believe everything my ex-wife tells you," he said.

She shook her head. Which subjects of Alice's discourse does he not care to have her believe? The analysis of Sandy's openhanded conduct of his affairs with other women? The certainty that by this token Myra must have known about these affairs? Or is it the more dramatic news that Alice herself had been one of those women, and that his willingness to accept this had led Ken to seek a divorce? Is this the subject, with its inevitable ramifications, on which he's displeased to have her trespass?

She looked at him, but his face was set in the grim lines that said subject ended. All right, back to the aberrant driving again.

But he got them there. Past the traffic streaming out of the city, over the inadequate bridges, along highways that worked less well than had been expected, finally on to the tree-shaded street leading to the white fence and spacious lawn she remembered from last time. The lawn was empty now, no small boys dashing for considerately hit balls, but Dianne was there, her face suffused with gentle pleasure as soon as they got out.

Simon would be right down, she said. He didn't like to keep them waiting, but this wasn't the easiest time of day. Always some hassle on the trip home, and then the phone messages, sometimes even people waiting, inconsiderate, really, you'd think they'd understand the pressures on a man just home from work. And then so important to him to have some time with the boys, that was what mattered most. He was changing now. They were going out to dinner—Simon told her, didn't he? But not to worry, their hosts expected them to be late, when wasn't he late these days? Anyhow, plenty of time for that half-hour talk Mrs. Berringer said she wanted. Meanwhile, a drink and something to eat? Oh, and maybe they'd like to come this way, past the flower beds—yes, a delight at this time of year, she was so glad they could get here before it turned dark.

All this was said in her soft, agreeable voice, while the wind blew at the wisps of hair curling over her forehead, and Margaret thought, lucky Simon. What every rising politician needs, standing between him and his inconsiderate public: the perfect sidekick.

The drinks were on the screened-in porch in back. Drinks, small sandwiches, paté, cheese. Plus a glimpse of the two boys, this time playing on a side lawn. Dianne handed each of them a plate. There must be plenty of servants to keep this big house going, Margaret supposed, but in deference to whatever disquiet servants might arouse in the egalitarian breasts, they would be kept largely out of sight. An invisible army. She had a vision of the little boys passing platters at dinner parties, while Dianne, face shining, would move serenely back and forth to the kitchen.

Dianne went inside now, to return with ice. Then she sat, facing the lawn. She'd called up to Simon; he'd said another few minutes. Meanwhile, wasn't it pleasant here? These wonderful spring nights, you wanted to clutch at every second.

More than pleasant, Margaret thought. Idyllic. Idyllic, that is, if you crossed out what was ahead, and also if you ignored Ken's face still set in its steely unease. She watched the boys, who were doing something intricate and energetic with a beach ball. "How old are they?"

Dianne smiled: one given a crack at talking about her favorite subject. "John's nine. He's the sensitive one. I guess every mother says that about her oldest. Imagine what it's like for their teachers, while mother after mother comes in: I have this deeply sensitive child. But in his case it really is true. He was born with a bone defect, one leg turning way out. The doctor said he'd be lame by twelve, but Simon wouldn't listen. His son lame! No way. That's Simon. If he sets his mind on something, nothing stops him. He got other verdicts and found out about some drastic massaging we could do on our own. We? Him, mostly. An hour morning and night. And it worked. Well, look—he's the one in the red shirt over by the lilacs. You can hardly notice a limp, can you?

"And Timothy's eight. His father all over. Eight years old and he organized a class protest last month. Something about where they had to play in gym period. He made speeches and wrote letters—the whole bit. I don't know why anyone put up with it," she said with shy pride. "Fresh kid like that organizing the whole school, but darned if he didn't pull it off. A natural politician." Dianne pushed the ringlets off her face, to have them spring back again in the breeze. "And he's fascinated by Simon's running for Congress. I thought he'd hate it, something to take his father away from the house even more, but no. He has a notebook where he's keeping tabs. This committeeman for, this one against, this one on the fence, we have to do some arm-twisting. Simon says that—Oh, good, there he is now."

Simon on the lawn with his boys: the prettiest of pantomimes, Margaret thought. Too far to hear, but instinct gave her the words. Hey, Dad, you really have to go out tonight? Sorry, kids, it's a must. But last night you said—I know, John. I hate it too. And the night before—Listen, Tim, you know what? This Sunday is all yours. The whole day. So if each of you figures out something special... It was all there: grievance, anger, tenderness, pain, affection. All in the mobile faces lifted to the man, the stormy gestures, the hugs he gave each of them before coming up to the porch.

Well, bring a dynamo into a group, and the complexion of the group changes. Something electric. Even Ken, by his stern gaze and set lips trying to dissociate himself, say he really wasn't here, even he sat straighter in the wicker chair. And Dianne gave an extra flutter as she passed the canapes, and Margaret took a longer sip of her highball than she had planned. Only Simon was himself. The boyish haircut, the big, square handsome face, the practiced smile: a man in charge.

And he didn't rush them. A dinner party was waiting for him someplace, a whole set of imperatives to propel him off this cozy porch and on to the next stop, but he didn't turn to Margaret and say, Let's get down to business. He poured soda in his drink and commented on the weather and said which route did they take coming up, was it through Green-lawn or did they come past that excavation for the new office building downtown, shameful really that the town board would allow a monstrosity like that. Then he said Ken hadn't been up here since that time two years ago when he and Dianne were thinking of doing some tinkering with this part of the house, well, the project wasn't dead yet, not by a long shot.

Then Margaret's turn. He was glad to see her. Times like this, it did people good to get together, exchange remembrances, air their thoughts about those who were gone. But besides that, anything special on her mind?

Margaret looked again toward the lawn, where another child, someone in a red shirt like John's, had joined the others. The ball game was now formalized: two against one.

"They're going to arrest my brother tomorrow," she said. "Everything points to it. I suppose after all this time I should be prepared, but I'm not. I keep thinking of him in one of those prison hospitals. Will there be other paralyzed men there too? Will they expect him to make his own bed? What kind of provision for therapy? Anyhow, why am I wondering, it wouldn't matter, he wouldn't hold out a month, a week. He'd find some way to do away with himself." She felt her hand tight on the chilled glass. "And I know you've both been wonderful, Ken and Simon, you've told the police everything. Well, not quite everything. Not about that hundred thousand dollars Sandy deposited. Money no one can get a line on. So I thought, if he was into something, some shady transaction, say, and someone was afraid he knew too much, or maybe he didn't come across with what he'd promised . . ."

"We've talked about this already." No kindness in Ken's voice.

With him too, Simon pointed out—his voice was gentler, but it came to the same thing.

"Oh, it's true. Neither of you knows anything definite, of course not. But if you could just put your minds to it once more. Come up with some hint. Maybe something Sandy said, or someone he was seeing. Ken especially." She turned slightly toward him. "Someone who came to the office, not a regular client, and Sandy gave an evasive explanation."

"You want me to think of everyone who came in?" Ken said coldly.

"I know it's asking a lot."

"It's asking the impossible."

"Hey, wait a minute," Simon said. "She just might be on to something. I know it's a wild card, but—"

"I've already given you the name of someone from our files," Ken told her.

"Well, it didn't lead to anything."

"Is that why I had to come up here, to answer a question you could perfectly well have asked in New York?"

"I think I understand," Simon said. "She figured if you were here, all of us together, I'd lend my weight." He put down his drink. "I am lending my weight. Her brother is the one taking the rap. You have to give her credit for trying."

"Would they really put him in prison?" Dianne said in a quavering voice. Margaret looked at her, the strained expression, the wayward hair, and she understood. The quaver is partly for her children. It is turning dark quickly—too dark, maybe, for the boys playing on a lawn. This must be the time she calls them in, checks on homework, settles fights, assigns TV privileges, hears grievances—the precious and closely monitored time before she turns them over to one of that invisible army. But she won't say so, not Dianne. She's too discreet, too much the perfect hostess to hint that she'd like to be engaged in some other activity than this conversation about whether a man she doesn't know might end up in prison.

"They sort of have to imprison him if they think he did it," Margaret said. "I mean, on the one hand, it's crazy, he couldn't by any conceivable terms be called a threat to the community. But on the other hand, justice demands it, doesn't it; you can't let murder go unpunished."

Dianne shook her head. Threat...justice...murder—not the kind of talk she was accustomed to on this pretty porch, with the wicker furniture and chintz pillows and fuchsia blossoms dangling from hanging planters. The idea of Sandy doing something shady, she just couldn't imagine it, she said softly.

"Even nice guys get mixed up in unwise transactions," Simon told her with quiet pedantry.

"And from all I've been able to find out, he always was mad for money," Margaret suggested.

Three heads nodded. "I'll buy that," Simon said.

"I'm not sure what an architect would do to get money out of line."

"Well, I imagine—of course Ken would know this better than I do—he certifies that some structure is okay when it isn't." Simon was still speaking with his calmly doctrinaire tone. "Or, conversely, he testifies that something could do with a whole new foundation when in fact it's structurally sound."

"Now that the two of you have it all sewed up, how do you know I wasn't in it too?" Ken stood so abruptly the wicker table shook. "I mean, if you're accusing Sandy, who can't defend himself, how about me?"

"Ken, relax." The same tone Simon would use if John or Timothy complained out of turn. "Nothing's final. Margaret's just seizing on anything. She's desperate—you can understand that."

"Well, I'm sorry about her brother, but as for the rest, I'm fed up. First she figures poor Myra must have done it, all that playing around of Sandy's with other women. Then maybe it's me, I must have had it in for him because three years ago Sandy and my wife had a thing—okay, you never said it, but what else was all that talk about? Now it's something called a shady transaction. No one knows exactly what the shade consists of, but it sounds useful, it's a theory, let's all hang on to it. Well, I'm not hanging. I think it's idiocy. It's what happens when amateurs barge in where they don't belong. Sandy was my partner for ten years. If he was getting money under the table, I would know about it." The incensed face turned to her. He was leaving now. He'd take the train. She'd probably be glad to drive home alone.

"Don't be dumb."

"Listen, have another drink first, I insist; we're not going to part like this." Simon meaningfully clinked the ice bucket—when he stopped they could hear the shouts from the lawn: Hey, Tim, throw it here. Timmy, to *me*.

Margaret looked past the screen. Did the boys know Sandy well? Did they like him? Were they upset about his death? She spoke lightly: one doing her part at the decompression.

"Sure they liked him, how could they not?"

"But they really didn't see him much," Dianne said with rueful eagerness—she also knew what was called for. "Not at all these past eight or nine months. Simon, now I feel awful. We didn't go to that big party he and Myra were having last winter, remember? You had some business appointment, and then, I don't know, somehow we didn't invite them..."

"How about Myra?" Margaret said. "Anyone see much of her?"

Dianne was still shaking her head. They didn't see Myra either. Such a shame. Oh, this just showed, the unbelievable things that could happen, you should never let family relationships slip.

"I guess no one really knew Myra," Margaret said. "Unless you wanted to count her maid."

"A maid?"

"You didn't meet her? She was from Bermuda. Sandy and Myra went there on vacation and Sandy ran into her working someplace and asked would she come to New York? And, surprise, she actually came."

"You never told me," Dianne said to Simon. "Maybe we should do that. All the trouble you have today getting dependable help. Though I suppose," she added softly, one willing to look at all sides, "you can go through the arrangements, the forms and money and everything, and then be stuck with a lemon."

"I don't think Myra was stuck," Margaret said. "The woman, Helene was her name, worked out very well."

"Listen. Maybe if she's looking for something now..."

"Afraid not," Margaret said, and sat back in one of the chintz-covered chairs. "She had some big inducements to go back home. She didn't really understand the nature of the inducements, they were unauthorized, actually, but it was all very tempting, and she went."

"And we never even talked to her," Dianne said. "You know, Simon, I sort of wish we'd told her where the funeral would be. A woman like that, after all she went through, she might have felt comforted by talking to the family.''

"Well, she did her talking to me," Margaret said.

"To you?"

"It was interesting," Margaret said. "She seemed a sort of deadpan woman, simple, almost, but once she got going she wasn't so deadpan about things that happened to her long ago. Well, one really traumatic thing, really, twenty-five years ago when she was a young girl.''

"That's what she talked about, her traumatic girl-hood?"

"Actually, she didn't just talk, she wrote out what she had to say. I mean, that event that was so important to her. Wrote it out before she left and then signed it and gave it to me.''

Dianne slipped the cover on the ice bucket—the smallest possible hint that she wished her guests would leave. "Goodness. Sounds almost, well, compulsive.''

"Yes, well, life sometimes makes you that way," Margaret said.

"You're pretty compulsive yourself, Mrs. Berringer." Simon was watching the boys.

"It's what you told me to be the first time I came up here. Go to it, you said.''

"I remember. My advice isn't always followed so exactly." Simon looked at his watch. "Dianne, would you entertain these nice people for me? I just remembered. I promised to leave some papers at Matt Howard's house by seven-thirty. Just take me a few minutes." He kissed Dianne on the back of her neck as he walked out.

Dianne blinked, but only for a second. Another talent: the ability to accommodate to whatever alteration in the social plans has been decreed. Would they have another drink? Or some of this paté? No, they must not think of leaving. They heard Simon, he would be really hurt. In fact, she herself needed them to stay—a barely perceptible sigh, as that obliging and collaborative mind slipped into another gear—so she could talk to Kenneth about the prospective renovation. Because they're really serious about it. They had a long talk, she and Simon. Even if he's elected, they won't move to Washington; this will remain their home. Goodness, they would not do that to the boys, especially John; take that sensitive child out of his school and neighborhood. So anyhow, what they're thinking of now is to add a deck outside and turn this screened-in porch into a second living room, what does Ken think of that?

"Depends what needs you're trying to fill," Ken austerely said.

Dianne looked with sweet earnestness from under the tendrils of hair. "Well, it would be nice to go from the kitchen right onto a deck when we were having cookouts. But there's something even more important. This second-string living room would be for the boys. Oh, I know, right now it looks as if they'll be playing out there forever. But they grow up so fast. And I heard Simon talking to them the other day. He said when he and his brother were in high school, their house was a kind of central meeting place. Permanent open house, sort of. Boys and girls, everyone welcome."

"Party land," Ken said.

"Exactly. And I saw John's face light up as if he were storing the information away for future use. It's funny. Timmy is naturally like Simon, but John is the impressionable one who consciously tries to emulate—there's nothing Simon says or does that doesn't have an impact. And if that's the way it'll be"—she put back her shoulders, a woman game for that ongoing party—"I want to be ready. Let them have their own place. Not in our living room, with the oriental rugs and antique pottery." She gave her rueful smile, as if to apologize for wanting to save her valuables from the partying of boisterous adolescents.

Ken murmured something about the size of the deck, and the two of them moved a few feet away in speculative talk. Glass louvers . . . cedar walls . . . benches . . . carpeting . . . all the details involved in altering a house to the end that the social life of young boys might emerge as a recapitulation of their father's.

When Margaret looked out, the boys were gone. Maybe, she thought, the game has shifted to that accessible lawn in front. Or maybe they've moved next door, where the man of the house, pressed for time like Simon, also preempts this hour for his children. Or more likely one of those unseen servants has spoiled the fun, said, Time to come in now, no, it doesn't matter what Mommy said, this is when you take your baths.

Ken and Dianne were still talking. While they were at it, some changes in the boys' bedrooms, Dianne suggested. Desk space. Bookcases. Stereos. Computers. "They'll be in high school before you know it," she explained with quiet pride. And then, "Oh, excuse me," because the phone in the next room was ringing.

Ken said nothing after Dianne was gone. He didn't come over to Margaret, but his face wore no special animosity either, as if the exercise of his own architectural disciplines had served to mitigate the anger on that other front. From somewhere on their right, the breeze carried the smells of a cookout, and from the left there was the faint ping of tennis balls—other families taking advantage of the insufficient daylight hours. Then another sound broke across the fragrant dusk. A woman shrieking. "No!" Dianne in a voice that had no right coming from someone with delicate good looks and a compliant manner. "No!" that unprecedented voice cried again. "He can't have! I don't believe it! No!"

Margaret put her hand on Ken's arm. "Let's get out of here," she said.

TWENTY

"AND THIS IS WHAT the deck would look like," Ken said. "If she ever should decide she wants the deck."

Margaret looked at the sketch on his drawing board: glass louvers, built-in benches, cedar flooring. They were in his office, where he'd asked her to come before they went out to lunch.

"Do you think she ever will want it?"

"I doubt it."

Then why did you draw it? She doesn't ask. She knows why. It comforts him. It's how he wants to remember that pretty fragile compliant woman. Not shrieking a useless denial into the unhelpful phone, but standing next to him on the porch while they contemplate appealing changes to her splendid house. Margaret walked around, stopping in front of the familiar drawings but not really looking at them. "She'll get married again. Dianne," she said at last. "That type always does."

"What type?"

"The perfect wife. Maybe take a couple of years, but there'll be another man in her life. Someone for her to take care of, accommodate to, make excuses for. Especially because she was so happy with Simon, there'll be another man."

Ken rolled up the sketch of the deck and put a rubber band around it. "What about the boys?"

"Little harder for them, I guess. Stepfathers never come easy. But if everyone acts right—and with Dianne running the show, everyone is sure to act right—they'll accept him, and then they'll like him, and then maybe they'll even love him.''

''What I meant was, what will they think about Simon?''

She sat down. Almost twenty-four hours later, and mention of the name still raises a lump in her throat. ''They'll think what everyone else does. What the newspapers told them. He was overworked, and through being under this terrific pressure from everything, he accidentally turned right when he meant to turn left, and he crashed through the fence around that excavation, and fell forty feet in a speeding car, and was dead by the time the ambulance got there.''

''Suppose he hadn't started talking about that excavation to make polite conversation to us—''

''He'd have thought of some other place. Maybe not so efficient, but he'd have pulled it off. Someone driving a car who wants to do away with himself can usually manage.''

''What about Dianne? Think she'll ever know the truth?''

''Not unless you tell her or I do. Ken, listen. Did I say anything to give it away?''

They walked into the room with the long table. An important room, suitable for important conversation. ''Only to the person you were trying to give it to,'' he assured her.

''Actually, none of it was the way I planned. I did envision what you said. A confrontation. Don't get angry—sort of a confrontation. But all that talk when we got up there about how the boys look to Daddy, they emulate Daddy, they want to be what Daddy is when they grow up... Brand that Daddy a murderer! I couldn't do it. Not to them or to her either.'' She started drumming her fingers on the Formica surface. ''Only thing, was it necessary?''

''What's that?''

''Branding him a murderer at all. He could still be alive. Throwing a ball to those kids. Kissing Dianne on the back of her neck.''

"And running for office," Ken said. "United States congressman, a murderer."

"But no one would know it was murder. Like the tree that falls in the forest when no one is around."

"Hey, don't knock it. All you said was what under the circumstances someone had to say."

She folded her arms on the table. "You really think that?"

"You'd better believe it," Ken said. He reached for a stray pencil before looking up. "Only thing, I still don't know how you found out he was a murderer."

"I told you everything in the car going home."

"You think you told me everything. You mumbled something about Bermuda and chambermaids, and then you cried, and then some more incoherent talk, and then you got really hysterical."

"Was that when you stopped for coffee?"

"And after that, you went to sleep."

"Not such good company, was I?"

"I've had better," he said.

"Ah. So you want the whole story. Start to finish." She watched him open a window, letting in fumes from cars and a blast from a driver across the street. Then he said the whole story would be a help.

"Hard to say when the start is. No, it's not. It's the day I go to Myra and you and Simon and say I want to have Sandy call me from Chicago."

"About that swimming pool," he said wryly.

"Yes. That visit all of you saw through after the murder. Except if one of you had been thinking about murder beforehand, if that subject had been on his mind . . ."

"Margaret, now what's your point?"

"I set things up for him," she said. "Gave him the necessary push."

"Look here. Quit blaming yourself. It's like what you said about suicide. If someone wants to do it, they manage to pull it off. So now tell me how you found out about him."

She turned around. A new set of drawings on the far wall. Views of a parking garage. Imagine: someone being creative, even poetic, about a parking garage. "You know what did it? The catalyst, as they say? Erica asked me to write up some case histories about women working off the aftermath of rape. She asked me, that perceptive girl, because I was depressed. She could perfectly well have written them herself, she or that snappy therapist, but they had this ingenious pact to pretend that—Well, that's another story. So anyhow, there I was thinking about what those women had in common. They all felt rotten about themselves; their self-esteem was way down. And they all had a hard time relating to the people they'd been closest to. And of course they all knew one way or another their lives had taken a decided turn for the worse. But three of them were in there fighting. They were using strategies—sometimes very inept strategies, but strategies of their own devising—to try to turn things around. But not that fourth woman. She'd given up. Just blocked it out. Only in the process she'd blocked out other things too. She lived in a place where no help was available. No help, but everyone knowing that as sexual property she was damaged goods. So what's the defense against that? You distance yourself from it. You cultivate that dry-as-toast impassivity that dissociates you, sets you apart. You exclude the world, and then get sore at it for—Listen, you must be starved. Should we go for lunch and I'll finish there?"

"Finish now," he said. "I want this lunch to be good."

"So I remembered I knew someone like that. Myra's maid. The woman who was with me when I found Myra. Well. A dead body on the floor of her studio. Someone you've been with, day after day, for almost a year. Only this woman, Helene, had no reaction. She didn't lose her head or scream or cry or even look upset. No affect, is what they call it. Know what I mean?''

He reminded her that he'd been married to a psychiatrist.

"Also, she told her landlady that something terrible had once happened to her. No details. Just terrible enough to balance in her mind a windfall I'll tell you about later."

He nodded.

"So as soon as I saw Helene as the prototype of this fourth case history, at that point, a lot of other things came into focus. "Like what?''

"Like—wait a second, I made a list before I came, I thought you might want to know."

"Good thinking," Ken said.

"Here it is. Item one, a clipping from a Bermuda newspaper of twenty-five years ago that Sandy had been keeping in his safe deposit box. Bermuda, incidentally, is where Sandy and Simon went with their parents for vacation. Anyhow, along with a bunch of small notices, the clipping lists one about a chambermaid in a hotel who was raped by an eighteen-year-old guest.

"Any names?''

"Not even any details. Myra figured Sandy had kept the clipping because of a write-up of a hospital dedication on the other side. She thought Sandy's father, who seems to have been prominent, or at least rich, had been the big donor."

"Okay. Nameless local girl raped by nameless young tourist. What else?''

"Item two—I'll try to give them chronologically, as I got them—item two is that hundred thousand dollar deposit."

"The one you started talking about last night as I guess a diversion for Simon, only I overreacted."

"You were right to overreact," she said. "It was a bum excuse for a topic. I was desperate. I had to keep talking till I figured out some way of introducing that maid that would not arouse suspicion in Dianne but would let Simon understand."

He said she rated an A on that one.

"Anyhow, item number three is a girl in Chicago, who—"

"Chicago. You really did get around."

"A girl Sandy loved and could afford to marry. He told her so. He said he expected to come into a mint of money, enough to maintain her in the style that was necessary to him and also to make the kind of settlement decency demanded for Myra. What number am I up to?"

"Four."

"Well, four is a talk with someone who went to high school with Sandy and Simon. Who were not real brothers, incidentally. Sandy never told you? Simon was adopted, and the relationship had the kind of built-in strains I guess that relationship always has. Or maybe that didn't happen till later. Anyhow, this classmate confirms what Dianne told us. The Fleming house was party land. Any time the high school kids wanted some fun, the Fleming living room was where they had it. But what Dianne didn't say, what Simon would surely not have told her, was that after the Fleming family came back from a spring vacation in Bermuda, the partying suddenly stopped. Everything verboten. House off limits. Also, social life outside the house seriously curtailed. Whole new set of stringent rules—the kind of thing that can seem like the end of the world when you're seventeen. This friend took for granted the crackdown was due to some disaster in Papa Fleming's life, business failed, marriage gone to pot, but he never heard of any. A rich suburb where everyone could be expected to know this kind of thing, but he never heard of any disaster. Just Papa suddenly turns sour on his boys."

"Okay. Lights out in the Fleming household. Go on."

She checked her list. "We now move up twenty-five years. Item five. Sandy and Myra go to Bermuda for vacation. Bermuda, that staid place, not the kind of resort you think a flashy fellow like Sandy will choose, even Myra doesn't think it, but he says Bermuda and they go and Sandy finds a woman who is willing to come back to New York as their maid. Why is she so willing? Largely because an apartment is part of the deal. A nice studio in a desirable building for which, lucky lady, her boss pays the rent."

Ken whistled, but all he said was she should go on.

"Let's see. Oh, the next is the fact, also confirmed by Dianne, to the effect that there are no visits between the brothers for eight months, which is roughly the time that imported maid is on duty. Simon sees to it that he and Dianne are unable to accept an invitation to Sandy's and Myra's party, and by the same token, Sandy and Myra are not on the guest list of any shindig at that sumptuous suburban house."

"Keep going."

"Only two more items, both about Helene. After Myra's death, she calls to inquire about a funeral. On Simon's orders, Dianne tells her there will be no public services. And last of all, an unknown benefactor suddenly delivers to her that windfall I was talking about. Namely, an airline ticket to Bermuda plus a sum in English currency equivalent to ten thousand dollars, with the explanation that it's a bequest from Myra's will."

"That money you said was unauthorized."

"Unauthorized because even in the unlikely event that Myra left ten thousand dollars to a woman who worked for her less than a year, there's no way a will can be probated and a beneficiary paid off within a week of death. But Helene doesn't know that, and in any case, why should she care? She does what the benefactor doubtless wants her to do, what he figured she would do, which is take the money and leave.'' Margaret took a breath.

"And that's it?"

"Isn't it enough?"

The phone rang; he picked it up and said sorry, Mr. Ash was out to lunch. Then he sat. "I think I see," he said after a long pause. "Is it your idea that when Simon was a young fellow, he raped a chambermaid in Bermuda, and that his father, due to considerable clout, was able to squash any reverberations down there, but that in order to chastise his son, he clamped down on that gala partying when they got home? A clamp that hurt Sandy as much as Simon. And is it your further idea that Sandy used this experience to needle his quasi-brother, so that years later, for instance, he got involved with a rape clinic, went so far as to design their office, just so he could get Simon into the mortifying position of having to represent women who'd been raped? But when Simon got more vulnerable because he was running for office and any indiscretion from the past could not just embarrass him but ruin him—Margaret, sit down, you make me nervous standing like that—do you think at this point Sandy saw his chance to up the ante and collect real money instead of sadistic gratification? And do you further suggest—God, I sound like one of those TV district attorneys—that to convince Simon he had the wherewithal to make the story stick, he brought up the girl who I assume is a girl no longer but the deadpan Helene, and did he threaten to arrange a meeting unless Simon came across? And then, according to your thinking, did Simon in fact come through with a preliminary payment, that mysterious hundred thousand dollars, but when he heard about your brother David's plans did he realize there might be a better way to get himself off the hook? And finally, at least I hope this is final, my throat is getting dry, is it your idea that to make sure he was in no danger from an accidental meeting with Helene, he arranged for a nifty plan that would get her out of the country on the double?''

"Ken, you got it. Terrific!''

"You did the legwork. Margaret, my God, what an incredible job.'' He leaned back contentedly in his chair. "Now where's the proof?''

"What do you mean?''

"The written statement you said Helene gave you that lays out the whole—''

"There is no written statement. I just said that so Simon—''

"Say that again.''

"I did it to fool him. And it did.''

"You mean, Helene never told you anything, you made up this scenario out of whole cloth?''

She couldn't sit; she was back at the window again. The tree at the curb was stirring lightly, a dance of the brilliant green, heart-shaped leaves. Under its canopy, two women stood with their baby carriages. "But Ken, knowing the same facts I did, you're the one who made it up.''

"That's different,'' he said flatly. "I was just speculating. Purely hypothetical.''

She was still facing the street. "It must have happened this way. I mean, look at any aspect of it. Any. Something significant must have happened in Bermuda, otherwise why would Sandy have kept that clipping? And that woman, the maid, must have been important to him, otherwise why go to all the trouble and staggering expense to bring her up from there and keep her in New York? And Simon must have known she was dangerous to him, that if she saw him she might recognize him, so that's why he never went to Sandy's and he wouldn't let her come to the funeral. In fact, at the funeral, now I think about it, he stayed out of sight till the doors were shut and the service began. To mention just three facts out of dozens."

"I haven't been exposed to so many assumptions since I read a biography of Shakespeare. We cannot know for certain, but Shakespeare's wife must have disapproved of his becoming an actor; he must have arrived in London in the late 1580's; his company must have traveled abroad during the plague years; he must have returned to Stratford for his mother's funeral."

"It's the way biographies get written."

"But not the way murder trials are conducted," he said.

"Do you see any holes in the story?"

Another pejorative pause. "Yes. For one, when this girl, well a woman, heard the name Fleming, didn't she connect it with what you say was her great trauma?"

"Not necessarily. Hotel maids don't need to know, are better off not knowing, the last names of handsome young guests who flirt with them. And afterwards, the Fleming clout must have kept everything hushed up, no mention of a name."

"Another convenient assumption." Ken looked briefly at her list. "Okay, here's one more problem. Sandy was due to stay in Chicago all that week. How did Simon cotton to the fact of the early return?"

"Because Sandy must have told him—Ken, don't look at me like that. I know for sure he called Myra, the girl in Chicago told me. And I bet he called you too, didn't he? I guessed it. That's the way he was—expansive about his love affairs and about everything else too. So all right, he calls his office, he also calls his brother with whom he has some complicated dealings—granted? And when Simon went to that site, at what he knew would be the right time, he must have been lucky enough to spot David's car, which gave him a chance to put David into the role of chief suspect and also, incidentally, to have David on the verge of firing the very agreeable man who takes care of him. Ken, any more objections?''

He spoke flatly. "How do we know Sandy was blackmailing his brother?"

Take it easy. Stay calm. He's the kind of man who believes in covering all the bases. "You said yourself that hundred thousand dollars was a first payment."

"That was a hypothesis. Now we need the facts."

"The facts," she said slowly. "The facts are that Sandy never made any bones about being jealous of Simon. Simon, the adopted son, the one who'd done the reprehensible act that queered the good time for everyone, for him to be pulling down the big money—"

"You have no real proof about that reprehensible act either," Ken said. "Nothing except a torn clipping and a problematic profile of a rape victim."

"A clipping he kept for twenty-five years in a bank vault," she murmured. "But no real proof. You're right."

"Also, there's nothing that irrefutably spells murder. Not a single piece of evidence to show that Simon had a gun, and drove at the appropriate time to that site on Long Island, and waited until your brother providentially drove off, and then pulled the trigger himself."

She frowned, remembering how hard it had been for her to accept the idea of David in that offensive role. Can she expect someone else so readily to slide Simon into it? No evidence, she admitted. Just what she figured was a plausible supposition.

"And finally, you can't submit a single fact to pin down Simon as Myra's murderer."

She had an overpowering desire to stop talking. Just to sit here, looking with honest appreciation at the duct stretched in brazen yellow across the ceiling, and the red formica table, and the blueprints, and against one wall, the glass cabinet with its miniature trees and glassy stream lending the required cosmetic touch to the model of a factory parking lot. "But we know that the old school friend told Myra the same story he told me. And it's reasonable to suppose she jumped to the same conclusion I did—don't say it, Ken, don't say it. Anyhow, we do know that right after he left she made a phone call saying she wanted to see someone. What ground do I have for deciding the someone was Simon? Well, we also know—Ken, this at least is a fact—Simon went to great pains to avoid an encounter with Helene. So why else in the middle of a work day would Myra take the wholly unprecedented step of telling her maid to go out for three hours, except that Simon must have said, Sure I'll come over and talk, but make sure no one else is around."

"And Simon comes over and hears that the threat once wielded by Sandy is now in Myra's little hands, and having had the foresight to equip himself with a gun, a different gun this time than the one he used on Sandy, he takes the necessary action—that your thesis?"

She nodded. That was correct.

"Margaret, you'd have some time with this in a court."

"I don't have to take it to court. You forget. Simon gave us the best proof of all that he preferred that it not go to court. Doesn't that clinch it?" And when he didn't answer, "Ken, doesn't it?"

He looked around at the drawings encircling them, as if to call on the verities, the irrefutable laws governing weight, stress, proportion, pitch, that governed his world. He liked things to be positive, he said.

"All right, I can make it positive. I can take this story to the police, they can check into everything. They'll send operatives to Bermuda to find Helene, and rehash that old story of a rape, and check the source of that money that was delivered—I doubt if you can turn ten thousand dollars into English currency without leaving a trace—and find the messenger who brought the money, and go over Simon's schedule for the time Myra was killed—all the details. And in the process John and Timothy will grow up knowing their father was a—"

"Don't do that," Ken said quickly. "Don't ever think of doing that." Then with his new expression—Margaret, you win—he looked up. "The only trouble is, you know your brother didn't do it, but he doesn't know you know, and also the police don't know. This way, he'll always have it hanging over him."

"No. I forgot to tell you. They found his gun this morning. They sent divers down at the bridge he thought was most likely, and there, embedded in the sandy bottom it was."

"He hadn't fired it?"

"That's right."

Ken was the one walking up and down now. "This whole experience—won't it leave him even more dispirited?"

"Just the opposite. I told you how he's been since the accident. Nothing to do with friends or work or any kind of service—just solitary brooding. Brooding, that did it—all day every day. Purest self-destruction. But with this case, he's been back in the world. One way or other, a participant. And guess what, he finds he likes it. This past year his college had been after him to run their investment trust for them. Exactly what he's trained for. So each time they called, he'd say no, that stubborn man, not interested, nothing doing. But this morning, just after he got the news from the police—oh, Ken, happy days—this time I actually heard him say yes. My brother may be ready to join the living."

"So that ties it up. Case finished."

"I surely hope so."

He was over at her side of the table. "Margaret, I didn't help you with the tying. I can think of three instances over the last few days. God, no four if you want to count the inquisition I put you through just now—four instances when I gave you unnecessary grief."

"Hey, don't knock it," she said. "All you said was what under the circumstances someone had to say."

"Then that settles it," Ken said. "Now let's go for that lunch."

Worldwide Mysteries provides the finest in mystery and suspense.

THE CASE OF THE FRAGMENTED WOMAN—Cleo Jones $3.50 ☐
After a voluptuous soap opera star is brutally murdered and an old friend becomes a suspect, a bored housewife finds more trouble than she bargained for when her investigations lead her to the killer!

FULL HOUSE—Shelley Singer $3.50 ☐
Private investigator Jake Samson is hired to locate a religious cult leader and a lovely devotee who have disappeared with a quarter of a million dollars.

THE WYCHFORD MURDERS—Paula Gosling $3.50 ☐
When investigating the murder of three women, Chief Inspector Luke Abbott is led down a prickly path of sexual obsession, drug abuse, jealousy . . . and his own past.

THE CAVALIER IN WHITE—Marcia Muller $3.50 ☐
When a valuable painting is stolen, Joanna Stark suddenly realizes that she is unwittingly concealing the very information necessary to recover the painting . . . and solve a murder.

Total Amount	$ _____
Plus 75¢ Postage	_____ .75
Payment enclosed	$ _____

Worldwide Mysteries are keeping America in suspense with spine-tingling tales by award-winning authors.

FINAL MOMENTS—Emma Page $3.50 ☐
Intuitive Detective Kelsey is faced with many suspects and alibis when a beautiful young divorcée is found murdered.

NIGHTMARE TIME—Hugh Pentecost $3.50 ☐
The disappearance of an Air Force major and his wife from the famous Hotel Beaumont throws Pierre Chambrun, the hotel's manager, into an intriguing investigation.

WHAT DREAD HAND—Sarah Kemp $3.50 ☐
Dr. Tina May thinks she will get some badly needed rest at a friend's cottage, but instead finds herself in a nightmare of witchcraft and grisly death.

BLOOD COUNT—Dell Shannon $3.50 ☐
Luis Mendoza and his LAPD colleagues face a varied, bizarre batch of cases, ranging from a mugging to a young girl's mysterious suicide.

Total Amount	$ _____
Plus 75¢ Postage	_____ .75
Payment enclosed	$ _____

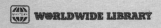 **WORLDWIDE LIBRARY**

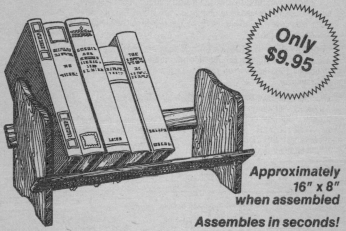

Worldwide Mysteries—keeping you in suspense with award-winning authors.

THE DEAD ROOM—Herbert Resnicow $3.50   ☐
When a murdered man is found in a dead room, an anechoic chamber used to test stereo equipment, Ed Baer and his son investigate the virtually impossible crime, and unravel an ingenious mystery.

MADISON AVENUE MURDER—Gillian Hall $3.50   ☐
A young woman investigates the brutal murder of a successful art director and comes to understand the chilling flip side of passionate love . . . and the lowly places to which the highest ambitions can fall.

LULLABY OF MURDER—Dorothy Salisbury Davis $3.50   ☐
A reporter investigates the murder of a famous New York gossip columnist and finds herself caught up in a web of hate, deceit and revenge.

IN REMEMBRANCE OF ROSE—M. R. D. Meek $3.50   ☐
An elderly woman is found dead, victim of an apparent robbery attempt. But lawyer Lennox Kemp is suspicious and discovers that facts are scarce and bizarre, leading him to believe that there is something sinister at play.
Not available in Canada.

Total Amount	$ _____
Plus 75¢ Postage	_____.75
Payment enclosed	$ _____

Please send a check or money order payable to Worldwide Mysteries.

In the U.S.A.	In Canada
Worldwide Mysteries	Worldwide Mysteries
901 Fuhrmann Blvd.	P.O. Box 609
Box 1325	Fort Erie, Ontario
Buffalo, NY 14269-1325	L2A 5X3

Please Print

Name: _____

Address: _____

City: _____

State/Prov: _____

Zip/Postal Code: _____

WORLDWIDE LIBRARY